14 Days

THE
SPUDDY

A lonely boy, a homeless dog and a kindly sea captain touch each other's lives in this poignant story of courage and devotion. When Andy, dumb since birth, was deserted by his mother and sent to live with relatives in a small seacoast town, he thought the world had come to an end. Sure, his father was good to him, but he was away at sea most of the time, small comfort to a beautiful nine-year-old boy who never learned to speak. Yet when he met "the Spuddy," a lonely, stray dog with spunk and intelligence to match his own, he began to understand love for the first time.

Frolicking on the moors, fishing on Skipper Jake's boat or just wandering along the rocky coast on a quiet afternoon, Andy and the dog developed the kind of affection that needs no words—and then it happened, the threat to their relationship, which leaves an indelible mark on the townspeople and the boy.

The Hills Is Lonely
The Sea for Breakfast
The Loud Halo
A Rope—in Case
Lightly Poached
About My Father's Business
Green Hand

THE
SPUDDY

a novel by
Lillian Beckwith

DELACORTE PRESS / NEW YORK

Library of Congress Cataloging in Publication Data
Beckwith, Lillian.
The Spuddy.
I. Title.
PZ4.B3968Sp4   [PR6003.E283]   823'.9'14   75-17599
ISBN 0-440-07681-1

*In memory of "the Spuddy,"
whose phenomenal intelligence
prompted the writing of this book.*

THE
SPUDDY

chapter **1**

WHEN Joe died Marie Glenn decided to say
good-bye to her home in the brisk little fishing port of Gaymal and take herself off to begin a
new life in Glasgow. All she was leaving behind was
her husband's dog, "the Spuddy," a thick-set gray-
black mongrel which he had brought home as a
puppy four years previously. He was called "the
Spuddy" simply because Joe had been in the habit
of describing anyone who was more than a little
astute as a "Spuddy," and when the dog had begun
to display a remarkable intelligence Joe had often
found himself saying, "He's a real Spuddy, that one."
So "the Spuddy" he had become. Despite his hy-

bridism (Joe used to say his coat looked as if someone had dipped him in a barrel of glue and then emptied a flock mattress over him) the dog had an air of self-assurance emphasized by an arrogantly held head and a long droop of a setter-like tail which, as he moved with his easy sauntering gait, swung from side to side with the stateliness of an ermine cloak.

The bond between Joe and the Spuddy had never developed into devotion on either side, for though he had housed him, licensed him and seen that he was well fed, Joe's feeling for the Spuddy was mostly an absentminded sort of affection, while the Spuddy, accepting that he had an owner but not a master and too proud to ask for that which was not offered, retaliated by according to Joe the forbearing protectiveness he might have bestowed on a child.

Joe had worked as a fish porter down at the pier and it was there that the Spuddy had loyally accompanied him on six mornings of every week with such regularity that people said the dog ought to be drawing the same wages as the man. And certainly the Spuddy proved himself useful. If anything was dropped into the harbor and needed to be retrieved Joe had only to call the Spuddy's attention to it and the dog would plunge in. Once he had saved a child who was in danger of drowning, and people had made a fuss and said he ought to have a medal, but since no one outside Gaymal got to hear of the rescue and since the townspeople quickly forgot about it there never was any medal for the Spuddy to wear on his collar.

Apart from the Spuddy's skill at retrieving, Joe valued the dog's company because he performed two self-imposed but important tasks on the pier. Firstly, he kept all loafing dogs from fouling the boxes of fish that were waiting to be loaded onto the trucks—a job he accomplished with snarling efficiency. He ignored their interest in the piles of empty boxes since these would all be hosed clean before being used again, but let any dog loiter too near the full boxes and the Spuddy would be on him instantly, sending him yelping for safety.

His second task was to keep the seagulls away from the newly landed boxes of fish, a task he performed with boisterous venom, for if there was anything in this world that the Spuddy had learned to hate it was the rapacious gulls. When, among the hurry and bustle of landing fish from the boat, the weighing and auctioning, the gulls converged upon the boxes of silvery fresh fish, the Spuddy would be there leaping with lightning snaps and spitting out feathers while he dodged the beaks that jabbed at him from all sides. He was responsible for many damaged wings among the local gulls, and once when he had caught the wing of a greater blackback and refused to let go, the gull had somehow managed to pull him over the side of the pier and into the harbor. But the Spuddy had held on, and while the fishermen and fishporters stopped working to watch, the contest continued amid a great splashing of water and a chorus of cries from the black-backed and spectator gulls. The battle lasted all of five minutes and then the Spuddy, his nose red with his own blood, swam back to the pier steps, leaving the dead blackback floating on the water and the harbor patterned with white gull feathers.

After Joe died the Spuddy appeared to go into semiretirement, and though he still visited the pier from time to time, he usually arrived in the late morning when the boats were at sea and the gulls, either hungry or gorged, had arranged themselves in a white frieze along the roof ridges of the sheds and shops that adjoined the pier. It was almost as if he had called a truce with the birds. He still went home for his meal each day as soon as the clock struck twelve, just as he had always done with Joe. He continued to sleep on the mat inside the porch, but Marie, who had been appalled when Joe had insisted on introducing the Spuddy into the household, had never learned to like the dog. For Joe's sake and because she considered it her duty, she still put the Spuddy's meal out every day, but not for anybody's sake, she vowed, was she going to take him to Glasgow with her.

"You couldn't keep a dog like the Spuddy in a room and kitchen high in a Glasgow tenement," she told her friends. "Not even if you wanted to"— which she certainly didn't.

She had made one or two halfhearted attempts to give him away, but most of the people of Gaymal felt that dogs were to be tolerated as playthings for the children only until the children were of an age to be packed off to school. Then the dogs became a nuisance and were disposed of quickly and without compunction. The few people who professed to like dogs acquired them as status symbols and were unlikely to give a home to a nonthoroughbred. Effie, one of Marie's neighbors, had summed up the problem with heartless clarity.

"What? Give a home to a beast that's as much an accident as a rabbit on the moors?" she had shrieked at Marie's tentative suggestion that she might take the Spuddy. "Indeed, if folks is goin' to be bothered with a dog then they want one that has a decent pedigree so that everyone will know it's cost good money."

Marie accepted the truth of Effie's statement. In those days, not long after the war, the fishermen of Gaymal were prosperous and they had to ensure that everything they possessed not only cost money but looked expensive. "You'll just have to have him put away before you go," Effie had insisted. But Marie, briskly matter-of-fact as she was, recoiled from the idea.

"I don't know indeed," she said, shaking her head. "Joe wouldn't have liked me to do that." The mention of Joe brought tears to her eyes.

"There's nothin' else you can do, is there?" pursued Effie, more gently though at seeing the tears. "Give him to one of the boats and get them to weight him and throw him overboard when they're well out to sea."

"It doesn't seem right, that," objected Marie hesitantly. "After all, the beast hasn't been much trouble. I think the best thing to do is just to leave him here. He's always been kind of independent and I daresay he'll make out." She paused, seeing Effie's lips tighten. "He'd get plenty of offal down at the pier," she resumed, "and the boats throw out plenty of food into the harbor he could get for himself. He wouldn't starve."

"If you leave him to wander 'round here folks will soon get fed up with him an' it won't be long before one of the boats takes him out to make an end of him," Effie told her. "You'd best just give him to the Cruelty an' then he'll be off your mind."

"It seems a shame," Marie's voice wavered.

Effie glared at her. "I'm no dog lover myself," she asserted, "but to my mind it's not so cruel to have an animal put away as it is to desert him after once givin' him a home." She turned toward her own front door. "But I daresay I might just as well save my breath to cool my porridge," she said as she inserted the key. "You softhearted folks make your own troubles, always takin' the easy way out." The door closed firmly behind her.

Back in her own kitchen Marie tried to make up her mind whether or not she was going to approach one of the skippers to dispose of the Spuddy. If she just left him and if what Effie had predicted was true then he would end up in the sea anyway. But at least, she told herself, when that happened she wouldn't be there and so have to feel guilty about getting rid of Joe's dog. In the end she decided to leave the Spuddy. She reckoned Effie was right about her being too softhearted.

The furniture van had left. The hired car that was to take her on the first stage of her journey had arrived. Marie settled herself in beside the driver, telling him she wished to get away as quickly as possible and giving an explanatory nod toward the Spuddy, who was hovering around as if awaiting the invitation to join her. As the car drew away from the curb, Marie turned to wave to the neighbors who had gathered to see her off. The car reached the end of the street and turned into the main road. The Spuddy stood watching it until it disappeared, and sensing the finality of his rejection, made no whimper of protest. After a few minutes he climbed to the top step of the empty house and lay down, staring along the street, his mixed-tobacco brown eyes shadowed with the fatalistic acceptance of his plight. The neighbors lingered gossiping for a while before returning to their own homes. The street became quiet except for the mocking echoes of gull cries carried in by a sea wind. With a sigh the Spuddy's head sank down onto his outstretched paws, but his eyes stayed wide and reflective, like those of a man mulling over future plans.

chapter **2**

WHILE Marie Glenn was speeding away from Gaymal another car was speeding toward the village. In this car there were again only two occupants, the driver himself and sitting beside him a boy about eight years old who stared out at the passing landscape with wide inscrutable eyes. The boy's name was Andy, but he could not have told anyone that, for though he was a good-looking boy, well grown and sturdy with curly fair hair and large eyes the color of fresh-cut peat, he was completely dumb. When people first saw Andy they tended to exclaim admiringly: "That's a grand-looking boy!" but when they realized he could not speak they would add: "Ach, the poor thing's a dummy!" And Andy, whose hearing was at least as good as theirs, winced at their pity as if it had been abuse. From the time he had been able to understand the speech of adults and become aware of his own affliction he had begun to feel excluded even from his own parents. His father was in the merchant navy and was away for long periods, leaving Andy and his mother on their own. But their being together had not brought them close. It was not that his mother displayed any lack of affection toward him; on the contrary, she was at times demonstrative. But Andy had been a beautiful baby, and when he had outgrown the toddler stage and his dumbness had become apparent, she started to feel a sense of outrage that her son should be imperfect. She had taken him to doctors and to specialists, all of whom assured her there was nothing physical to account for Andy's lack of speech, but as time went by and he showed no sign of improvement her resentment toward him grew, and it was only intensified when he was refused admission to the local school.

She tried teaching him herself, coaxing and cajoling sometimes for hours on end and mouthing simple sounds for him to imitate until tears of frustration filled her eyes at his continued lack of response. To Andy it seemed that the more she tried, the less able he was to respond. He felt as if his body were empty of sound, that there was no mechanism to articulate no matter how hard he tried. Seeing her frustration he developed a dread of her lessons, feeling sometimes as if he were freezing inside whenever she made him sit down on the stool in front of her and commenced her repetitive mouthing of sounds. It was not so distressing when she taught him other things like lettering, and he shared her delight when eventually he was able to produce the large misshapen capitals that spelled his name; but having taught him to write his name, except for reading stories to him, her interest in lessons waned until there was only fitful instruction on any subject she found easy to demonstrate, like the hours of the clock and the value of coins.

Her loss of interest in lessons appeared to be accompanied by a similar loss of interest in the boy himself. Often now, she seemed distracted, and instead of taking him with her when she went shopping she began leaving him with a neighbor. Andy knew that his muteness embarrassed her and that he was a terrible disappointment to her. He tried hard not to mind that she was away from him so often or that in the evenings when she was home he was usually left to sit quietly drawing in a corner of the room while she entertained her friends.

His mother was thankful for Andy's interest in drawing and she made sure that he always had an ample supply of materials, but even though she often complimented him on his skill, only his father's praise and criticism were really meaningful to Andy. It was only his father who knew about boats, and Andy almost always drew boats. Great liners, cargo boats, sailing boats, fishing smacks, even dinghies—he drew them all, and when he was not actually drawing boats he drew the moody sea and wharfs and harbors complete with seagulls.

He had seen liners and cargo ships when he and his mother had gone to the docks to wave good-bye to his father's ship. He had seen fishing boats and a great variety of other craft when they had spent holidays in Aberdeen with his granny. But now there was no longer a granny in Aberdeen and so no more holidays there, and the only water he could get near was the pool in the park and the sluggishly flowing river which separated it from the town. But the beautiful shapes of boats and the restlessness of the sea had stamped themselves on his mind and he continued to draw from memory, content in his private world while he listened to the lively chatter that went on around him. Sometimes, looking up, he would think how much prettier his mother was than all the other women in the room and sometimes he wondered if, beneath the gaiety, she was, like himself, longing for his father to come home on leave so that they could all three be together. There came a time, however, when Andy noticed the number of friends being entertained had dwindled, until there were only two or three and finally only one, a man, whom Andy did not much like. When he came his mother insisted on Andy's going to bed.

When the telegram arrived announcing his father's imminent arrival, instead of grabbing Andy's arms and dancing around the room with him, his mother rushed upstairs and began packing suitcases. Coming down again, she said in reply to Andy's look of bewilderment, "I'm going away for a bit." Her voice was strained. She gave him no further explanation but told him not to go out until his father arrived, and added that there was a cold lunch prepared for them both in the pantry. Then she put an envelope beside the clock on the mantelpiece. "See your father reads that when he comes," she told him. She was frowning in an abstracted way and her eyes were bright. As she moved past him Andy put a hand on her arm and looked at her imploringly. "I can't stay, Andy," she said in a tight voice. "It's no good. I just can't stay." His hand slid down to his side. "Be a good boy," she said, giving him a quick hug. The door closed behind her and she was running down the garden path and out to the car where a man was waiting. She did not glance back or wave to her son who stood forlornly holding aside the curtain watching his mother go.

Even when his father arrived and enveloped him in a huge hug Andy did not break down but only pointed to the letter on the mantelpiece. With a quizzical glance at Andy as if he suspected a joke, his father took the letter and sat down to read it. After he had read and reread it he stood up and put a hand on Andy's shoulder. "Your mother's gone away for a wee whiley," he said thickly. "I expect she told you. It's your granny, she's not keepin' so well. I daresay she'll be back soon." He didn't look at Andy as he spoke. "Now I'm just going upstairs for a wee kip and when I come down again we'll put on our best bibs and tuckers and go out somewhere, eh?" He was too distressed to see his son's anxious eyes following him out of the kitchen.

Andy stood desolate. He had wanted his father to talk to him, to admit that his mother had left them for someone she liked better and not try to fool him with a lie about Granny. He knew what had happened and he wanted his father to share their mutual knowledge and their grief; he felt they should have been able to comfort each other. His shoulders sagged. It seemed that even in this moment of crisis his dumbness was still a barrier; that even his own father accepted that an inability to speak meant a similar inability to understand and even feel or share emotion. Andy got out his paper and crayons but he did not want to draw. He wandered into the pantry and looked at the food but he had no desire to eat. He had no desire for anything—not even to go out as his father had promised, because of a fear that if they left the house it and all the other familiar things would not be there when they returned. Not knowing what to do with himself, he went at last and sat on the bottom stair, hugging his knees and listening for a sign of movement from his father.

When his father did come down, determinedly bright and talkative, they went out despite Andy's reluctance to leave the house, and for the next six weeks of his father's leave they did more things together than they had ever done before. There were trips by rail and by bus, walks in the country, fishing, meals in restaurants, all filling Andy's days with so many new experiences that at night he was too tired to brood for long.

The day came when his father began preparations to return to his ship and once again Andy was overcome with hopelessness.

"Tomorrow," his father said in reply to Andy's questioning glance. He knelt down, and putting an arm around the boy, he went on. "I've fixed up for you to go and stay for a little while with your Aunt Sarah and Uncle Ben. You've never seen her, but she's seen photographs of you and she's taken a real fancy to you." He felt the tension in the boy's body and his arm tightened around him. "And there's your Uncle Ben. You'll like him. He doesn't draw boats like you but he builds them. They live at Gaymal where there are plenty of boats. You'll be able to go down to the pier whenever you like and draw as many as you've a mind." He looked into Andy's eyes. "You'll like that, won't you?"

Andy nodded and managed a faint smile.

"Aye, and you'll be able to get on board one or two of the fishing boats for a trip if you've got good sea legs, which you ought to have, boy, seeing you're the son of a sailor." Andy knew his father wanted him to show enthusiasm so he responded as best he could. He dreaded the idea of leaving home and going to live with strange people even if they were relatives, but he knew there was no alternative.

"There's a car coming for us both tomorrow and I'll ride with you part of the way," his father continued. "I wanted to come with you all the way and see you settled in but my leave's been chopped a bit. The idea now is that this car will take us to

the docks where my ship is and you'll be able to
see me go aboard before you set off for Aunt
Sarah's." Andy nodded and again forced a faint
smile.

"So off you go up to your bedroom and pack up
anything you want to take. Mrs. Peake next door
is coming in to pack your clothes and things, but
you'll be wanting to take your paper and crayons
and a good few of your sketches, eh?"

As Andy went slowly up the stairs to his bedroom his father stood staring after him, asking
himself whether it would be more heartrending to
have a son who could confide in words his fear and
dejection rather than one like Andy who could
only convey it by the slump of his body and the
anguish in his eyes.

At the docks Andy watched his father stride up
the gangplank of his ship and turn and wave
before he disappeared from sight. The driver took
Andy's arm, insisting that they continue their
journey if they were to reach Gaymal before dark.
Stoically Andy returned to the car. The driver was
a compassionate man and talked brightly in an
attempt to distract the boy from his grief. He
pointed out everything that could possibly interest
him; he stopped and bought him sweets, but
though Andy was determined not to cry, the driver
could see that he was taut with pent-up emotion
and that his attempts to cheer him up were having
little effect. Fearing he might make some clumsy
remark that would crack the control Andy was
keeping over himself, he lapsed into silence and
was relieved when, shortly after five o'clock, they

entered Gaymal and pulled up in front of a house three doors away from Marie Glenn's former home.

The Spuddy still lay on the top step of the empty house, having returned there after seeking out the dinner Marie had conscientiously left for him in his bowl beside the coal shed. Marie had always put his dinner beside the coal shed and the Spuddy would watch her doing it although he always waited until the church clock struck twelve before he would approach and start to eat. Always, that is, unless the church clock happened to be slow, for it seemed his own sense of time was more accurate than mechanical time. If Joe ever spotted the Spuddy eating his dinner before the clock struck he would switch on the wireless to check the time so that he could report to Danny, whose responsibility it was to regulate the clock.

The Spuddy watched the car arrive as he had watched every other activity in the street since Marie had left. He saw the boy get out and be greeted by a plump, busy little woman wearing a flowered apron over her blue dress; he saw them go into the house for a while and then come out again, when the driver got into the car and drove away, leaving the boy and the woman standing on the pavement. The woman moved toward the house, calling to Andy, but he had noticed the empty-looking house and the Spuddy lying there alone and ran after her, pulling at her sleeve while pointing toward the dog. The Spuddy pretended not to notice as the woman, pausing to explain, shook her head disapprovingly in the Spuddy's direction. She disappeared inside, gesturing to the boy to follow, but Andy paused for a moment. With his hands grasping the pointed railings that divided his Aunt Sarah's garden from her neighbor's he leaned over and stared at the dog until the Spuddy's head came around and he returned the boy's stare with a long interested glance.

chapter 3

ANDY'S first thought on entering Aunt Sarah's kitchen was how much the room was like its owner. Both kitchen and Aunt Sarah were small and clean and bright. There were white curtains at the windows which matched her hair, and just as the fire in the open grate crackled busily as it burned, so did Aunt Sarah's tongue crackle as she bustled about. The table was laid for tea and there was a smell of kippers coming from the stove.

"You like kippers, do you, Andy?" Aunt Sarah asked briskly, and Andy nodded affirmatively. He had no appetite but he did not want to risk being questioned by this sharp-tongued little woman.

"And so does your Uncle Ben," she told him. "Though the Dear knows you'd think he'd be sick of the sight and smell of them, working so close to the kippering yards as he does. Still, they're good kippers we get hereabouts and I doubt there's better fish in the sea than herring when all's said and done." She put some plates into the oven. "Your Uncle Ben will be home any minute now, so you'll just come upstairs with me and I'll show you where you're to sleep." She picked up one of his suitcases and started up the stairs. Andy picked up the other and followed.

"There now," she said, opening the door of a small prim room. "How will that do you, d'you think?" Her mouth closed tightly on the question and Andy missed the smile in her eyes. He looked around and nodded, doing his best to appear grateful. It was a nice enough room, he conceded, but it wasn't like his own. The unfamiliarity of it almost broke through his control and he was glad when his aunt hurried away, reminding him firmly as she went that Uncle Ben would be home soon and that he liked to sit down to his meal as soon as he came in, so would Andy please just wash his hands and then come down. He could do all his unpacking later. Andy went to the bathroom, splashed his face with cold water until he felt more composed and went downstairs.

"This is your Uncle Ben now," announced Aunt Sarah, and almost immediately the back door opened and his uncle came in. Uncle Ben was tall and thin with undisciplined gray hair and a roughly shaven, sea-scoured face. On seeing Andy his blue eyes lit up and he lumbered forward to give him a warm handshake, and he nodded and smiled and told Andy how welcome he was and how nice it would be for him and Aunt Sarah to have someone young about the place. Aunt Sarah was dishing out the kippers, and just as Uncle Ben appeared to be running out of words of welcome she ordered them to sit down to their tea before it got cold.

Andy ate three kippers, or rather there were the remains of three kippers on his plate when he had finished his meal; but when he had thought his aunt and uncle weren't looking he had put some of the kipper flesh between two slices of bread and butter and slipped them into his pocket. He also hid two drop scones.

Since his aunt had explained that the Spuddy had been abandoned he had resolved that he himself must try to feed and look after the dog, and he estimated that if his aunt regularly put as much food on the table as she had this evening he would not have much difficulty in providing for the Spuddy.

After tea, while his aunt was washing the dishes, he slipped out into the evening dusk and sped quietly toward the gate of the empty house. The Spuddy watched him come. Not knowing for certain whether or not the dog was savage, Andy tore a piece of crust from the kipper sandwich and held it out, and when the Spuddy ignored the offering he opened the sandwich and waved it about, hoping the dog would be drawn by the appetizing smell of the fish. Since the Spuddy had eaten his one meal of the day, he was not hungry and refused to display any interest. All the same he was intrigued. The Spuddy had never thought of himself as a child's dog. Children were noisy and excitable and he preferred to avoid them, but though he could recall young boys trying to cajole him with soft words or to command him with curses, the patient, mute overtures of this boy baffled him, and he watched him, making no movement except for a flick of one ear as he saw him unlatch the gate, sidle through and advance tentatively up the path toward him. Andy held out the sandwich but still the Spuddy refused it. The boy's beseeching expression changed to one of disappointment. He put the sandwich and the two drop scones on the ground beside the Spuddy and retreated a step or two, but still the food was ignored. He ventured closer again, holding out a hand, palm outstretched, hoping the dog would sniff it, realize it was the hand of a friend and perhaps give it a lick of acceptance. The Spuddy looked at the hand and looked away again. He was not in the habit of licking hands, let alone strange ones; it would have been too much like an act of submission. To Andy the Spuddy seemed to be spurning his offer of friendship. He slumped down on the bottom step, looking up at the dog in the gathering dark, waiting for some reciprocal gesture of comradeship, and when it did not come his head dropped forward until it was resting on his arms, and his shoulders began to shake with the sobs that had for so long been wanting to escape from his body. Only then did the Spuddy weaken.

Moving down to the bottom step he sat down and laid a paw gently on the boy's neck, glancing about him as he did so as if he were afraid someone might witness his unwonted display of tenderness. He need not have worried. By now it was quite dark and there was no sound in the street until a door opened and Andy heard his aunt calling him.

chapter **4**

WHEN his son was six weeks old skipper Jake's wife announced that she must take the baby home to show him off to her family. "Home" to Jeannie was the home of her parents, a croft in the outer islands. The home Jake provided for her she always referred to as "the house." Jake accepted her announcement impassively. Jeannie was forever making excuses to visit home. Either her father or mother was ailing and needed her or there was to be a wedding in the family or a relative had just had a baby. In fact Jeannie's relatives made so many demands on her time that in the three years they had been married Jake doubted if she had spent more than six months with him. It hurt him that she wanted to be away from him so much of the time and he had hoped that when the baby was born she would become more attached, if not to himself, then to the home he worked so hard to give her.

As he came through from the scullery into the kitchen where Jeannie was ironing he was pressing a towel against his newly shaven cheeks, and only his eyes betrayed his unhappiness. There were times when Jake thought he ought to put his foot down about Jeannie's frequent absences but he knew in his heart he never would. She was so fair and young and slight and he was so big and swarthy and had such an intimidatingly gruff voice that he was fearful of appearing a bully in her eyes. So he erred on the side of overindulgence, giving her everything she asked for and never complaining of her lack of interest in him.

"Is the baby old enough to travel?" he asked, trying so hard to keep his voice gentle that it sounded almost meek.

"Surely," returned Jeannie as she guided the iron over the sleeves of a tiny jacket.

"It's just that I've heard folks hereabouts sayin' a baby's not strong enough to take the fresh air until it's six months old," he persisted, the gruffness edging back into his voice. "D'you not believe in that yourself?"

Jeannie tossed her head. "Indeed I believed that when I was younger because that's what the old folks say. Now the nurse says the baby's ready to take fresh air after about two weeks. After all," she added, "it isn't as if it's the wintertime yet."

Jake went over to the cot in the corner of the kitchen, and lifting the coverlet, gazed down at his sleeping son. His sad, tight mouth relaxed into a tender smile. Was he going to see as little of his son as he did of his wife? he wondered bitterly, and looked across at Jeannie, who with her back to him was still ironing. She had once seemed so shy and desirable with her clear smooth skin and glossy hair, but soon after they married he noticed her shyness had given way to an almost vixenlike quality; and though her complexion and hair remained as attractive as ever, he rarely saw her other than as she was now, in slippers and a robe with her hair in curlers. He let himself wish that she would dress herself up for him when he came home on weekends, but she never did. When he went away to sea on Monday mornings her hair was in curlers and when he came home on Friday nights it was still in curlers. For only about two hours on a Sunday was her hair unconfined and then, because she was going to church, it was hidden under her hat. However, this was not all that disturbed him, for it seemed that she found an awful lot of housework to do on weekends when he was at home, and while he admitted it was nice to know he had a clean, shining home, he would have preferred it to be a place where he could relax away from the constant swing of the sea: a place where he would be greeted by a neatly dressed wife prepared to share with him the comfort of their own fireside and where a few of the neighbors might drop in late in the evening for a wee dram and a "wee crack" and a discussion of the week's fishing. Like most fishermen he had a strong streak of romanticism, and when he was first married he had dreamed of the weekend respites from the discomfort of the boat: of returning and opening the door of his welcoming home to call, "I'm back, Jeannie!"; of finding her in his arms; of lifting her up and carrying her to the kitchen. But even before he had touched her she had seen the eagerness in his eyes and had evaded him. She "didn't like that sort of thing," she had rebuffed him. "It was soft." Now on weekends he returned either to a listless greeting and the bustle of housework, the moving of furniture that she was unable to handle by herself, the careful treading over newspapers that covered the constantly washed floors; or else, too frequently, to a house that was clean and shining but was cold and empty, and there would be a note on the table saying, "Have gone home—mother not keeping well."

At first she had stayed away only two or three weeks at a time, but then her absences grew to months and he realized that except for financial support there was little else she wanted from him. He wondered if she wanted what any man could give her, since island girls had a reputation for making their first duty the well-being of their parents. No matter what other commitments a woman might have, she had from childhood been so indoctrinated with the belief that her loyalty was to her parents and to the homestead where she herself had been born and reared that she cleaved more naturally to them than to her husband.

Gently Jake replaced the coverlet over his son. He cleared his throat. "I'd like to see a fair bit of the boy, Jeannie," he said.

"And when would you see him anyway?" Jeannie taunted. "With you away at the fishing all week it's precious little you see of your house, let alone your son."

"But, Jeannie!" he expostulated. "I've to earn money for us, haven't I? An' how else would I do it except for the fishin'?" He knew just how much money he had to earn to keep up with Jeannie's whims. She tired of things so quickly, forever demanding change, and he reckoned they had bought enough to furnish three homes in the time they had been married. Only he knew how he hated to have to call out his crew in weather that made other skippers comment: "It's only greed or need that would make a man go out to sea on a day like this."

Jeannie shrugged. "Well, what sort of a life d'you think it is for me here all by myself with a man only coming home on the weekends and him only wanting his bed then."

"But the other wives are the same," he pointed out. "A fisherman's wife knows what to expect before she marries him."

"Well, I can't help it if I like company," she retorted. "It's what I'm used to."

"Can you not make friends with the other women?" he asked. "They'd be company for you."

"Ach, they're that proud," she said defensively. "They're not my own folk."

"Aye, right enough they're not," said Jake resignedly. "But all the same I'm sayin' I'd like to see my son growin' up and there'll not be much chance for me to do that if you have him away at your parents' as much as you have been yourself. I'm askin' you not to stay away so long."

"That'll depend on how my father's keeping." Jeannie's voice sparked at him like sticks on a newly lit fire. "He wasn't keeping so well in my mother's last letter," she added. She thumped the iron down and started to gather up the pile of clothes.

Jake looked at her, dismayed as always by her apparent renunciation of him, but he was too proud and thought of himself as being too inarticulate to plead with her further. He opened a cupboard and took out some tools.

"Which is the shelf you say wants fixin'?" he asked her in a tired voice.

chapter 5

ALL that night the Spuddy lay on the steps of his former home, but when the first fingers of light reached over the shoulders of the hills he got up, stretched himself and sauntered away down the street. Andy, coming out of his aunt's house after breakfast, was disappointed not to see the dog and decided to go and look for him. Since he did not know his way about Gaymal, Andy had no idea where he should look but nevertheless he set out, and since all Gaymal roads led inevitably toward the harbor, he eventually found himself on the pier.

He stared in wonder. He had visited docks with his father, but busy and exciting as they had seemed to him, he now thought of them as being landlocked and dull in comparison with the spectacle of Gaymal. There was so much sea everywhere, so much sky and color and movement, and he could only stand letting the sights and sounds and the smells of the harbor envelop him. He forgot his intention of looking for the Spuddy; forgot the ache of depression that had been with him during the past few weeks. He even forgot for the time that he was dumb, since everyone was so busy and there was so much noise that people tended to gesture rather than talk.

Here were boats galore: herring boats landing their catches, launches loading supplies, the lifeboat swinging at its moorings; and at the end of the pier the steamer was hauling up its gangplanks, preparing to leave. Its raucous siren seemed to Andy to be lifting the upper half of his body from the lower half, and he pressed his hands over his ears to deaden the noise. Passing fishporters threw him friendly grins and Andy grinned back ecstatically. He picked his way among all the fish boxes, trolleys, barrels, hoses and ropes that go to make up the impedimenta of a fish pier, his shoes scrunching on pieces of crab shell or skidding on fish that had been pulped to slime by the wheels of the trucks, until he reached the end of the pier.

The steamer was well away now, leaving a wake like a discarded shawl as it sailed into a misty rainbow that arched itself across the distant islands. Andy watched until steamer wake and rainbow vanished behind a gauzy screen of rain, when, suddenly realizing that the rain was now sweeping in over the pier and that he was getting wet, he ran for the meager shelter of a high-piled stack of fish boxes, where he waited until the shower had passed before continuing along a path between more stacks of fish boxes which brought him into the boatyard where his Uncle Ben worked.

As his father had predicted, Andy had taken an immediate liking to Uncle Ben. He wasn't sure about his Aunt Sarah, since to him she appeared forbidding with all her scuttle and sharp-tongued splutter, but Uncle Ben was slow-speaking and smiling-eyed and was more given to acknowledging his wife's continued chatter by nodding his head than by saying anything. Andy's impression was that when Uncle Ben was not eating he had his pipe in his mouth, and except for his initial welcome, the only time he had spoken was when he took his pipe out of his mouth to refill or relight it. He had said little then but his voice had been gentle and the words comforting, so that Andy experienced the same warm, safe feeling he knew when he was with his father. He thought that some day, when they knew each other better, he might even show Uncle Ben some of his drawings.

Andy found his uncle working on a fishing boat that was winched high on the slip: a boat that had hit a rock, his uncle explained, and needed to have several planks renewed. She'd been lucky, his uncle told him. If the weather had worsened, the boat could easily have become a total wreck before the lifeboat reached her and the crew could have lost their lives. As he was speaking, his uncle's hands were caressing the boat's side with as much tender-

ness as a mother smoothing a crib sheet over a
sleeping child. Andy, who had never before seen
anything bigger than a dinghy completely out of
the water, was overwhelmed by the sheer size of the
underside of the boat. Standing beneath her and
letting his eyes run along the generous curve of the
bilge, the sweep of the hull into the keel, the sweet
run of the seams, he thought how beautiful she
was. Uncle Ben, who had been observing him, took
his pipe out of his mouth to say, "Aye, a boat's a
beautiful thing, boy," to which Andy replied by
running his own hands along the planks and smil-
ing rapt agreement. He knew now that no longer
would he be content to draw boats; he wanted to
go to sea and he wanted to go in a boat just like
this one he was admiring.

The church clock striking twelve reminded them
it was time for their dinner and in the leisurely
way of a devoted craftsman Uncle Ben put away
his tools. Together they left the slip, climbed up to
the quay and made for home. As they turned into
the street the first thing Andy saw was a large van
parked outside the empty house and men unloading furniture from it. Where's the Spuddy? he
thought in a panic, and was angry with himself
for having forgotten his intention of looking for
the dog. Andy dawdled, letting his uncle go in
front of him. He stood by the gate gaping at the
activity. Foolishly he had let himself think that the
house would remain empty; that the Spuddy
would continue to visit and sleep there and so be
accessible to further overtures of friendship. But
new people meant complications. New people

might have a dog of their own or they might dislike dogs altogether, and what would happen then? It was at that moment he saw the Spuddy.

The Spuddy had spent the morning doing his usual rounds of the pier and the kipper yard but when he had heard the clock strike twelve, habit had turned him in the direction of his former home. He was not expecting to find that his meal had been put out for him but he thought he might just as well make sure. When he saw the furniture van and strange people going in and out of the house he realized he was unlikely to be welcome there but he felt he could risk slipping around to the back to see if his bowl was in the accustomed place beside the coal shed. It was, but it was empty of everything except a few drops of rain and the lingering smell of yesterday's food. He licked it more to assert ownership than for the meat-tainted moisture, but even as he did so a red-haired woman appeared and amid a shrill scream of invective hurled a stone which hit the path beside him.

Ruffled but still dignified, the Spuddy retreated to the other side of the street and at what he judged to be a safe distance he sat down to keep an eye on the proceedings. As he did so there was a clang against the curb a few feet away from him. It was his empty bowl. The Spuddy was still sitting there, half obscured by the bulky van, when Andy spotted him. Immediately he ran toward him, and putting a gentle hand on the dog's head, crouched down and let his arm slide down until it was around the dog's neck. The Spuddy's response was a cursory lick on the ear which might have become more fervent had not the red-haired woman emerged from the house to scream at Andy not to encourage the beast. She wasn't going to have it hanging around her place, she yelled, as she reentered the house and shut the door. Andy, catching sight of the empty bowl in the gutter and guessing why it was there, knew that he had to do something. As he retrieved the bowl he heard his aunt's voice scolding him for his slowness in coming for his dinner. With an encouraging pat on the Spuddy's head, Andy left him and followed his aunt inside. When the meal was over and she had cleared the dishes away he showed her the Spuddy's empty bowl, mutely asking her for scraps.

"Indeed no!" she declared firmly. "I'm not giving you food to take to that dog. He should have been put away before his own folks went away, and it's only a matter of time before he's put away anyway." She put her hands on her hips and looked at Andy. "If you go tempting him to hang 'round here you'll upset the neighbors, and I won't stand for that. Anyway," she went on, "the more you tempt him, the more likely it's you yourself will be the death of him. Aye, you, Andy," she stressed, seeing his look of consternation. "The woman that's moving into the house was here taking a cup of tea with me earlier this morning and she canna abide dogs at any price, she was telling me. She's that nervous about them, she says, and if the Spuddy still comes 'round now that she's moved in, her husband's going to complain to the police." She gathered up the tablecloth. "Aye, and then something will have to be done about getting rid of him." She went to the back door, shook the crumbs from the cloth and coming back said less severely: "The best thing you can do for that dog, Andy, is to keep away from him and make sure he keeps away from you." Out of the corner of his eye Andy saw Uncle Ben nodding sad confirmation.

Aunt Sarah watched Andy dejectedly tuck the empty bowl under his anorak and go outside.

"I wonder what he's up to now?" she asked.

Her husband shook his head.

"I've got to be firm," she defended herself. "We can't let him go upsetting the neighbors."

"No," Ben agreed.

"It's a shame, though." She looked out through the window to where Andy was unlatching the front gate. "I hate to do it, seeing the way the poor boy must be feeling." She took up her sewing. "Maybe when he's been here with us a bit longer we could get him a puppy of his own, eh, Ben?"

"Aye," Ben nodded again. "Maybe that will make him happy." His voice was dubious and there was a deep frown between his eyes.

chapter 6

THE moment Andy saw the Spuddy again his dejection became resolution. The Spuddy and he were going to be friends, and friends must look after each other. It wouldn't be easy—that much he knew—but if only he could keep the Spuddy fed and unharmed until his father came on leave he was certain his father would find some way of ensuring that Andy could keep the dog. Sadness descended on him as he wished, as so often before, that he could correspond with his father; that he could read and write like other children of his age so he could both send and receive letters. But when his father was at sea their communication with each

other was limited to picture postcards with lots of
x's printed clearly on the back which his father
posted whenever he was in port. In reply Andy had
only been able to add more x's together with a pain-
stakingly printed "ANDY" to his mother's letters
and sometimes give her one of his drawings to
enclose.

Shaking off his despondency, Andy approached
the Spuddy, and showing him the feeding bowl,
tried to entice the dog to follow him, but the
Spuddy, used to verbal invitations and instruc-
tions, was reluctant until Andy's explicit gestures,
aided by a renewal of invective from the red-haired
woman, persuaded him to accompany the boy.
Before leaving the house Andy had checked the
money in his pocket, and money being something
his mother had made sure he was familiar with,
he reckoned he had enough to be able to buy at
least two and perhaps three days of food for the
Spuddy, and today being a Saturday it was only
three days before he was due for another week's
pocket money from the sum his father had left for
that purpose.

Pausing outside the butcher's he looked in at the
window but he thought the butcher looked har-
assed, and loath to risk adding to his harassment
by trying to convey by signs what he wished to
purchase, he chose instead to go to the general
store, where it was relatively easy for him to point
to a can of dog meat and a can-opener, hand over
the money and skip away. If he was aware of the
mystified shopkeeper coming to the doorway to
observe him further, Andy gave no sign, and

together he and the Spuddy raced toward a promising-looking huddle of sheds which he had noticed earlier in the morning. Here Andy felt sure he would be able to find a quiet corner where he could stand guard while the Spuddy ate his meal.

The sheds, he discovered, were situated within the kipper yard itself, a place where it was obvious the Spuddy was completely at home. It was in fact the Spuddy who led Andy to where two small, disused sheds abutted to form a reasonably secluded spot, and, watched closely by the Spuddy, Andy set the bowl on the ground, opened the can and tipped the contents into the bowl, pushing it toward the dog and nodding vigorously as he did so. The Spuddy regarded the boy in the same dubious manner as a shopkeeper might regard an urchin who has offered him a five-pound note to change. His glance dropped to the food and his nose twitched. With diminished uncertainty yet still without complete conviction his glance returned to the boy. Andy pushed the bowl nearer; he lifted it up and held it close to the dog's nose before putting it down again and only then did the Spuddy, with a dignified swing of his tail which Andy interpreted as a gracious "thank you," begin to eat. Crouching with his back against the wall of the shed Andy smiled.

The next thing he must do for the Spuddy, Andy resolved, was to try to find a place where the dog might sleep unmolested at night. While Andy was disposing of the empty meat can and while he washed the dog's bowl under the tap on the pier he thought about his problem. One of the empty sheds where he had fed the dog was a possibility, but where and how would he get sacks or some form of bedding to cover the damp-looking earth floor? When you were unable to speak it was difficult to indicate even the simplest things you wanted. How was he to mime to strangers his request for bedding for a dog he was not supposed to have? All afternoon the boy and the dog roamed Gaymal but when teatime came Andy had still found neither bedding nor a cozier alternative to the shed for his companion.

The evening dusk was thickening, and since his aunt had said that he must be home by dark he knew the time had come to leave the Spuddy. Clapping his hands he gestured toward the kipper yard but the Spuddy stayed beside him. He tried stamping his feet; a pretense of kicking and of throwing. He tried dodging and hiding but the Spuddy was not to be diverted. Feeling like a traitor Andy at last picked up a stone, and throwing it so as not to hit the dog, he made what he hoped was a menacing rush toward him. The Spuddy was surprised but not deterred. Andy grew desperate but it was Uncle Ben coming home from a visit to the barber who solved the problem for him. "Way back, boy!" he commanded the Spuddy. "Way back! You mustn't come near this place. Go!" His voice was quietly authoritative and the dog, understanding at last, turned away and loped off in the direction of the kipper yard.

The following day was Sunday and Uncle Ben volunteered to show Andy around Gaymal. As they turned the corner into the main road Andy was delighted to see the Spuddy apparently waiting for him, but unsure of his uncle's attitude toward the dog he dared only to make discreet signs to him to follow them. However, when his uncle took the path that wound up toward the open moors, the Spuddy, becoming increasingly sure of his welcome, began bounding along beside them. Andy glanced anxiously up at his uncle from time to time, but he seemed not to mind the dog's presence and even remarked at one point that he was a "real nice dog and it was a shame someone didn't take to him and give him a home." But when the time came for them to return for their dinner Uncle Ben's voice was firm as he commanded the Spuddy to "Get away now! Get away!" Obediently, after a reproachful glance at Andy, the Spuddy turned and went slowly in the direction of the harbor.

After dinner, with the scraps saved from his own plate in his pocket and with the feeding bowl inside his anorak, Andy again set off in search of the Spuddy.

"See that you are back by four o'clock," his aunt commanded him. "It's church tonight and we have our tea early."

He found the Spuddy wandering among the piles of fish boxes on the pier, and when he saw Andy he appeared uncertain whether or not to come forward and greet him. After his treatment of the night before and again this morning Andy could not blame him. He put the scraps into the bowl, set it down and waited. Slowly the Spuddy came to investigate, and liking what he found, licked the bowl clean. Andy patted him, wishing he could explain, and in return the Spuddy licked his ear. It seemed they were friends again, but when it was nearing four o'clock and he had to face the task of sending the Spuddy away, Andy felt sick. He waited until they were approaching the kipper yards before he turned and pointed toward them. He clapped his hands and pointed again emphatically. The Spuddy sat down and made no effort to follow him further.

chapter 7

MISERABLY Andy wondered if the Spuddy would ever come near him again and as soon as he awoke next morning his mind was busy with plans. He would explore the moors and hills beyond the village where perhaps he might find a cave the Spuddy and he could use as a hideout. Andy would have to return to his aunt's house each day, but if he could make a good bed for the Spuddy in the cave he might stay there and he should then be safe and snug during the milder part of the year.

Downstairs he indicated to his aunt that he would like to take his lunch with him, and she

was quick to understand and approve. Uncle Ben
wasn't at home for lunch except on Saturdays and
Sundays, an arrangement which suited her to
perfection, since she always found plenty of housework to do and liked the day to be free of inter-
ruptions so that she could get on with it. Never
having had children of her own she had become set
in her ways, and the prospect of having to endure a
child around the house for much of the day had
at first made her want to refuse the request that
she should give Andy a temporary home. But the
thought of his need had overcome her reluctance.
"We all have our crosses to bear," she told her husband with a righteous sigh, but the jolt of concern
she felt when she saw Andy arrive, with his big
watchful eyes shadowed with grief and tiredness,
made her realize she was going to find him no cross
to bear.

After Andy had gone to bed that night, she had
sat down beside the fire opposite her husband, who
was reading the paper. Taking up her sewing, she
had begun jabbing at it so clumsily that she
stabbed her finger with the needle. At her exclama-
tion Ben looked up and saw that the eyes of his
normally brusque, undemonstrative wife were
bright either with tears or anger. She caught his
look.

"Fancy a mother being able to do that to her
child, Ben," she said. "Just fancy." And the normally placid, virtually monosyllabic Ben surprised
his wife by saying explosively, "She's a monster,
that one!"

Andy pleased his aunt now by showing her he

expected to be away for most of the day. She cut up a pile of sandwiches, added half a dozen cold sausages and a couple of slices of cake and then she went to a cupboard under the stairs. "Here now, Andy," she said, returning with a haversack. "This will be useful for packing your sandwiches into. It was left here by a fellow that was on a walking tour of the hills and he didn't want to be bothered taking it back with him." Andy watched with pleasure as she put the food and a cup into the haversack. "You'll get plenty of drinking water on the moors," she told him as she helped him to slide his arm through the strap. "There now," she said. "Off you go." Again Andy saw only the tight lips and missed the warmth in her eyes. He bounded upstairs and got the Spuddy's bowl, which he had brought home the previous evening hidden under his anorak, and putting it into the haversack he thought, This is splendid. Just the thing for a couple of explorers.

Andy was relieved to find the Spuddy waiting and for a moment his spirits soared. Was the Spuddy really waiting for him? he asked himself. After what must have seemed to the dog Andy's rough treatment of him, had he after all understood and trusted him as a friend? As he walked toward him the Spuddy sat watching, cautiously assessing the boy's approach. Andy saw the dog's ears twitch, the tail begin to wave, and most comforting of all, the eyes brighten with welcome. Love and gratefulness surged through Andy. He began to feel wanted again and he bent down and

let the Spuddy lick his ear before they raced off
happily toward the open moors.

With the September sun taking the sharp edge
off a wind that really belonged to winter and with
the heather springy under his feet, Andy reveled in
the space and freedom of the moors. He had never
seen such vastness. He had never been so close to
such craggy, somber hills or, when he turned his
back on them and looked out across the sea, never
seen such splendid horizons. He plodded on, fear-
less with the Spuddy for company, but he did not
find a cave. There were rock-sheltered hollows and
boulder-roofed crevices but the former were open
to the sky and the latter were slimy and boggy and
Andy guessed they would stay that way no matter
how much bedding he might gather and put into
them.

He carried on with his quest, diverted only
when he found himself confronting a herd of
suspicious-looking highland cattle or when a rabbit went bounding away from his path. The
Spuddy displayed only a passing interest in the
rabbits, and Andy, thinking that Aunt Sarah might
soften her attitude toward the dog if he provided
the occasional rabbit for dinner, tried to urge the
Spuddy to give chase. The Spuddy sat and watched
Andy's signs with curious attention but he made no
move to go after the rabbit. A little disappointed,
Andy walked on, but before he had gone more than
a few yards he noticed that the Spuddy was not following him. He turned around to see him still sitting
where he had left him. Beckoning him to follow, he

walked on again, but still the Spuddy remained
where he was. Wondering if he was sulking, Andy
patted his knee coaxingly and beckoned more emphatically, but still the Spuddy would not move.
Andy went back, and patting the dog's head, urged
him again to follow, and when that had no effect he
examined the dog's paws, thinking perhaps he might
have cut himself on a splinter of stone. He could
find nothing wrong, and thinking to examine him
more thoroughly, took off his haversack and laid
it on the ground.

Immediately the Spuddy stood up and nudged
the haversack with his nose. Then he sat down
again and fixed Andy with a hypnotic stare. Andy
stared back, whereupon the Spuddy again stood
up and nudged the haversack. Though knowing
nothing of the Spuddy's rigid adherence to a
twelve o'clock dinner time, Andy understood that
the dog seemed to be indicating he wanted food;
and as the fresh air had keened his own appetite,
he looked at his watch wondering how near dinner
time it was. Seeing that it was five minutes past
twelve he sat down on a convenient thicket of
heather, his back against a boulder which sheltered
him from the wind. He opened the haversack, and
putting half the sandwiches and half the sausages
into the feeding bowl, placed it in front of the
Spuddy, who gave an appreciative wag of his tail.

Once they had eaten, the Spuddy was again
eager to follow, and subsequently Andy learned for
himself that at twelve o'clock the dog expected to
be fed and that he made known his expectations

by refusing to obey further orders until he was satisfied.

Continuing his search for a cave, Andy at last came across something he thought might suffice until he could find something better. It was really not a cave at all but only a low fissure between opposing slabs of rock which leaned together so that in the apex a roof of boulders had been trapped, leaving an opening in the shape of an inverted "V." Andy had to go down on his hands and knees and crawl inside and once there he could only just sit upright, but seeing that it was dry, he decided it would have to do. He set about gathering autumn bracken and dry mountain grass, filling his haversack again and again and emptying it onto the floor of the cave, and when he thought he had gathered enough to make a good bed he tested it himself. Finding it tolerably comfortable, he invited the Spuddy to lie beside him; and content yet alert, the Spuddy settled himself down. Andy lay listening to the hissing of the wind backed by the faint murmur of the sea, and as his eyes grew accustomed to the dimness he could discern the tiny outcrops of crystal among the rocks close above his head, so that when he half closed his eyes they sparkled like tears on the ends of his lashes. His eyes closed.

When he woke, the sun was hovering above the mainland hills and out at sea he could make out the outlines of the fishing boats converging on the harbor. He knew it was time for him to return home but first he had the task of convincing the

Spuddy he must stay in the refuge he had prepared for him.

It was difficult at first, the Spuddy being determined to follow Andy, but eventually he seemed
to understand, and as a reward Andy took out the
two pieces of cake from his haversack and put one
in the Spuddy's bowl. Then he hurried away,
glancing back every so often to make sure the
Spuddy was not following him. The third time he
looked back he was worried because the Spuddy
had moved away from the cave entrance, but then
he saw that the dog was not being disobedient but
was only seeking a better vantage point from
which to observe him. The last time Andy looked
back he saw the Spuddy had made his way to the
top of a high boulder and there, silhouetted
against the evening glow, was watching him leave.

chapter **8**

THE next morning, the Spuddy was waiting for Andy in what was to become their regular meeting place in the village, and again they made for the moors. When they reached the cave Andy was relieved to see that though there were remnants of bracken scattered outside the cave as if the Spuddy had remade his bed several times before it was to his satisfaction, inside the bedding was compressed into a round nestlike hollow. Andy pointed to the nest and patted the Spuddy before they carried on exploring and climbing over the shoulders of the hills, stopping sometimes to drink from the sparklingly clear streams or to paddle or skim stones into

the cold, hill-shadowed lochs. There was no difficulty this time in persuading the Spuddy to remain
behind when it was time for Andy to return home,
though just as he had the previous evening, he
insisted on leaping up onto the boulder to watch
the boy's departure.

The friendship between the boy and the dog
deepened steadily. Every morning the Spuddy
would be waiting for Andy, and when they were
not roaming the moors and hills they were down
at the harbor. It seemed to Andy that the days
raced by with the speed of the small wind-chased
waves he liked to watch rolling past the end of the
pier, and he was so captivated by the kaleidoscopic
pageantry of Gaymal that he had little time to
dwell on the crisis that had brought him there.
For the first few weeks after his arrival he had
looked every morning to see if the postman had
brought him word from his mother—perhaps a
picture postcard like those his father sent him
with lots of x's on the back to let him know she
still loved him, but as the weeks became months
and there was still no sign from her he began to
accept that either she had forgotten him or she
wished him to forget her. If he could not make
himself forget her he did at least succeed in opening his eyes to the affection that was being offered
to him in his new surroundings.

In addition to the Spuddy's devotion he had his
Uncle Ben, who made no secret of the warmth of
his feelings; and even Aunt Sarah, whose testiness
had at first unnerved him, began to reveal the tender side of her nature. She bought him more

crayons and more paper. She fussed over his health, and she began to worry about his lack of education, complaining to Ben that he had been wickedly neglected; she rowed with the local schoolmaster when he refused, because of Andy's affliction, to take him into school as a pupil, and when the darker evenings brought long hours indoors she determined that she herself would be Andy's tutor. Confiding this intention to a friend who also happened to be the school janitor, she induced him to "borrow" some lesson books so that she could teach Andy to read and write. Despite a scolding tongue, she displayed not only a natural ability to teach but also an astonishing patience with the boy, and stimulated by his keenness to learn, she tended to ignore most of the chores she normally felt compelled to do in the evenings so as to devote the time to Andy and his studies. The result of all this was that at the end of three months Andy found he could write to his father giving him the glorious news that if his father wrote a letter in return he would now be able to read it for himself.

During the day, Andy and the Spuddy spent hours down at the pier, mingling with the fish porters and watching the comings and goings of the boats. His eye was becoming trained to the lines of the boats and to their different responses to the sea, so that he could recognize each boat long before it reached the harbor. He knew most of the crews and was accustomed to being thrown a rope to hitch around a bollard or being told to bring a hose or even being called aboard to collect the empty pop bottles to take to the grocer with the instruction that he could keep the "penny backs" for himself. Andy was glad of the "penny backs" because they helped him to buy more food for the Spuddy to augment the scraps he saved from his own meals. Uncle Ben helped too by saving his own scraps, and if Aunt Sarah ever noticed the total lack of food on her table at the end of their meals she made no comment. As long as Andy did not offend the neighbors by allowing the Spuddy to hang around the place, she felt it right to hold her tongue. After all, she conceded, maybe a dumb boy needed a dumb friend, and at least the dog kept Andy out all day so that he wasn't constantly under her feet.

After a lingering autumn, winter howled in with wild sharp-toothed winds that scraped the skin like a steel comb. The hills which had been snow-capped became snow-shawled and soon snow-skirted; the pier puddles were skimmed with ice, and fishermen and porters flapped their arms across their oilskinned bodies, trying to keep warm during the minutes of inaction. Andy, snug in the thick sweaters his aunt knitted for him and in the "oilies" she had bought for him, began to worry anew over the Spuddy. He knew that the cave was too exposed to make good sleeping quarters for his friend during the winter, and when one cold but dry morning he noticed the Spuddy's coat unaccountably wet he went up to the cave to investigate. To his dismay he found that the bed he had made for the Spuddy was wet when he pressed his hand into it; when he pulled away all the bedding he saw that the ground underneath was little more than a bog. He gathered more bracken but the bracken itself was wet after the winter rain, and though the Spuddy seemed content enough to stay there, Andy could not sleep that night through worrying about the problem of shelter for his friend.

A few nights later there was a heavy blizzard and Andy found the Spuddy waiting for him in snow that was up to his belly; his ears were drooping and snow from the last flurry was still melting on his coat. When he tried to follow Andy he stumbled, and Andy knew the dog was sick. In desperation he resolved to go and see his Uncle Ben and somehow persuade him to help find a safe, warm place for the Spuddy to sleep. Down at the boatyard Uncle Ben watched Andy's passionately expressive mime with complete understanding, and after feeling the dog's hot nose and cold ears he led them to the far corner of the workshed where there was a great pile of wood shavings and cotton waste. Andy looked at his uncle with grateful comprehension and began to arrange the shavings into a nest which he lined with cotton waste. Even before he had finished, the Spuddy, without waiting to be invited, stepped into the center of the hollow, turned around twice and settled himself down. For three days the Spuddy hardly stirred from his new bed but lay there showing little interest in anything, even food; and Andy, fearing his friend might die, stayed around the boat shed, rarely leaving it except at his uncle's insistence.

On the fourth day, when the Spuddy saw Andy, he got up out of his bed to greet him. On the fifth day he was prepared to accompany him down to the pier and on the sixth day Andy was overjoyed to find the Spuddy waiting for him in the usual place near the main road. It was as well that the Spuddy had new quarters, for now that winter had come in earnest Aunt Sarah had forbidden Andy to go up on the moors alone. He and the Spuddy still went to the moors, but only on Sunday mornings and then in the company of Uncle Ben. The rest of the time they confined their wanderings to the harbor or to the paths and fields around the village, and when evening came Andy would escort the Spuddy to the boatyard and see him comfortably settled in his warm bed.

chapter 9

FOR skipper Jake and the crew of the *Silver Crest* the fishing season had proved a disastrous one. It had begun with a broken con-rod in the engine which kept them tied up at the pier for close on two weeks, and when that was repaired there had followed a run of bad luck which included fouled nets, a seized winch and gear damaged by heavy seas. When at last they managed to get a good spell at sea they found the herring shoals elusive, and instead of *Silver Crest* coming into port with fish holds so full that skipper and crew felt justified in taking a few hours rest and relaxation, she was arriving with a meager cran or two, which necessitated their turning around right after unloading and going back to sea to search for new grounds to set their nets, perhaps snatching only two hours' rest out of the twenty-four. Once one of the highest earning boats in the port, they had dropped to one of the lowest. The morale of the crew was at an all-time low and they were bothered by the superstition that the bad luck which was dogging them might yet bring worse catastrophe. But Jake dismissed their fears. Despite discomforts and disappointments he would allow nothing to affect his driving ambition to catch fish —more and more fish to earn more and more money for himself and his crew. And since Jeannie, his wife, was away from home visiting parents, Jake was also goaded by loneliness—loneliness and the recurring pain in his stomach that only hard work or deep sleep could dull.

Before he had met Jeannie, Jake, like most Gaymal fishermen, had been a heavy drinker, spending all his weekends ashore in the local hotel bar downing whisky after whisky, and when the pain had first started he had drunk even more whisky in the hope of alleviating it. Eventually it had driven him to see his doctor.

"You'll have to keep off the drink," the doctor warned after examining him. "I can give you medicine but medicine can't fight the damage the whisky's doing you. It would be different if you took better care of yourself, but ach!" The doctor shook his head. "You fishermen are all the same. You abuse your bodies all week, working like galley slaves, going without sleep and bolting great wads of stodgy food, and when the weekend comes you're away to the bar and pouring whisky into your stomach as if it was an empty barrel with holes in the bottom."

Jake had intended to heed the doctor's warning but Gaymal offered only two places where an unmarried man ashore for the weekend could find company and relaxation. They were the bar and a district up at the back of the kipper yards known locally as "Chinatown," where the itinerant "kipper lassies" had their quarters. Jake had nothing against the kipper lassies; indeed he preferred them to the local girls who, he considered, suffered too much from what he called the "I want disease," but not being by nature a wenching man he had settled for the bar, and since neither the Gaymal bar nor its customers welcomed teetotalers Jake had continued his drinking. Continued, that is, until Jeannie had come into his life.

From the day he had first seen her behind the counter in the local paper shop he had wanted her for his wife. Her smallness and primness delighted him and he liked to observe her pretending to frown at the teasing remarks of the fishermen while all the time, the enamored Jake was sure, she was really finding it difficult to restrain her demure little mouth from breaking into a smile. He thought that she was about half his age and he wondered if she would think him too old for her, so he was both astounded and delighted when she responded to his first tentative approaches; and when, after they had known each other for about two months, she agreed to accompany him on a visit to his sister in Glasgow, he felt the time had come for him to ask her to marry him. As they wandered along the city streets Jake intentionally edged her toward the windows of jewelers' shops and suggested with stumbling diffidence that he should buy her an engagement ring. She had declined at first as he had expected her to, but noting the sparkle in her eyes when she studied the rings in the window, he could see the temptation was strong, and when he pressed a little she soon yielded. He was earning good money at that time and the ring they chose was an expensive one; so also were the coat and jersey and skirt which she fell in love with and which he, in a glow of devotion, insisted she should have. What did it matter if he spent in a single night what had taken him a month to earn? He had a boat, hadn't he? And there were plenty more shoals of herring in the sea waiting to be caught.

The change Jeannie had brought into his life had been at first dramatic. In her company he found it easy to stifle the urge to drink, and during their courtship and the early weeks of their marriage and even during her first two or three absences from home Jake steadfastly renounced his visits to the bar with the result that not only was his pain less constant but his whole body reacted with a renewed vitality that reminded him of his youth. When Jeannie's visits to her parents became more frequent and more prolonged, Jake, disillusioned by her feelings for him and hating the emptiness of the house at weekends, relapsed into his former ways, beginning by drinking himself into a confusion of thought that he hoped he might mistake for happiness and culminating at closing time when he staggered home from the bar to drop on his bed in a stupor of intoxication.

In an effort to deaden the pain he thought of his wife's pale face, framed, as he liked best to recall it, by long tresses of her fine hair; and, as drowsiness teased him, he saw that her face was floating on the sea and her hair had woven itself into a net—strong net—fishing net, in which several replicas of her face were caught, and as the net was hauled in through the swirling water to break surface, there were hundreds more replicas and the hundreds became thousands and were no longer faces but herring—the "silver darlings": huge bursting netfuls of them pouring in a writhing, leaping, coruscating stream over the side of the boat and into the hold. Jake tried to clear his befuddled brain. If ever a fisherman needs to woo sleep he does not do so by counting sheep going through a gate but by counting herring: baskets and baskets of herring, cascading into the hold. How many? Again and again Jake tried to estimate, but perversely, as always, sleep overtook him before he could calculate the worth of the catch in hard cash.

chapter **10**

IT was in the early hours of a Monday morning after just such a heavy weekend that Jake, gray-faced and bloodshot-eyed, came down to the boat. The crew glanced at him with concern before turning to grimace at one another but they waited until they were gathered in the fo'c'sle and Jake was still in the wheelhouse before they commented on his appearance.

"A drink's a drink," burst out the youngest member of the crew indignantly. "But the skipper's killin' himself with it."

"It's that wife of his that's killin' him if anybody is," supplied another. "She knows fine he goes on the sauce whenever she's away from him. But she won't stay, not her."

"He's too good to her, that's what's wrong," put in the cook.

"It's just not decent the way she leaves him," said the youngest crew member again. "If she was mine I'd take my belt to her."

"Island women!" exclaimed another. "That's them all over." The speaker was an east coast man and he found the islanders utterly baffling.

"It's a bloody shame!" the young man continued. "He's a damn good skipper an' I don't like to see him made so little of by a woman." He frowned. "Particularly now he has the child," he added.

It was the oldest member of the crew who corrected him. "It's herself has the child," he said quietly. "An' I'm thinkin' there's little Jake will get to see of him now she's got away with him."

As he spoke there was an ominous clanking noise. The engine slowed, then ceased altogether. They rushed up on deck to see the skipper coming out of the wheelhouse.

"Take the boat!" he shouted at the man nearest to him. "That blasted engine's done the dirty on us again." He ran quickly down to the engine room. The old man looked at the cook. "That's it, then," he observed. "It seems as if our bad luck's not done with us yet."

After an hour of so of wrestling with the engine Jake managed to coax enough power for them to labor back into port where a worried-looking engineer was waiting for them on the pier. Together he and Jake inspected the engine while the crew waited gloomily wondering how long they were going to be delayed. The engineer came up on deck followed by a glowering Jake. "Not before midnight," he was saying as he wiped his hands on a bunch of cotton waste. "Not a hope." As one man the crew set off in the direction of the bar.

For Andy also the day had begun bleakly. That morning Aunt Sarah had told him of a new schoolmaster who had come to Gaymal—a master who was not only willing but anxious to have Andy as a pupil, and it had been arranged that he was to start school the following week. His momentary delight at the news was immediately overwhelmed by dismay: if he had to go to school every day, what would happen to the Spuddy? It would be all right in summer when the days were long, but in winter there would only be the lunch break, since it would be dark when he came out of school and Aunt Sarah was strict about his being home before dark. His misery was intensified when, calling in at the boatyard, he found Uncle Ben, who, after much apologetic head shaking, had warned him that his boss was insisting that the workshed where the Spuddy slept must be cleaned out and all the shavings and waste disposed of before the end of the week. There was to be no bed for the Spuddy at the boatyard anymore. Andy had gone to Aunt Sarah to try a last appeal, boldly taking the Spuddy to the house and pointing to the small shed at the bottom of the garden where she kept her gardening tools; but she, already having heard from her husband that the boatshed had to be

cleared, had steeled herself to resist Andy's
entreaty. Even if she were willing to risk upsetting
her neighbors by giving a home to the dog, she
told herself that the Spuddy was too big a dog to
have around her small neat house, and she knew
that were he to be allowed in the garden shed it
would not be long before Andy and her husband
would prevail upon her to have him in the house.

Pottering miserably around the pier wrestling
with his problems, Andy was there to witness the
unexpected return of the *Silver Crest*, and anxious
to know the cause of it he ran down to watch her
tying up. Of all the boats coming in and going out
of the harbor Andy thought the *Silver Crest* the
most beautiful in shape and the best cared for.
Empty or loaded, he thought, she rode the sea as
easily as the gulls or as serenely as the swans he
used to see on the river near his home. At her
mooring, if the sun happened to be shining, her
varnished timbers looked golden against the oily
green of the water. She was the boat he most
wanted, if ever he could go to sea, to be allowed to
sail in and yet, despite his admiration and despite
the fact that he was welcome aboard every other
boat in the harbor, Andy had never set foot
aboard the *Silver Crest*. Firstly, owing to the poor
fishing season *Silver Crest* had rarely been in the
harbor for more time than it took to unload, and
secondly, Andy was afraid of skipper Jake and his
rough voice. Ever since the day when he had been
sitting on a fish box sketching the *Silver Crest* on
the back of a letter he had composed to his father
and Jake had been angry with him, Andy had kept

his distance from the boat. On Jake's behalf it must be said he was exasperated by the complete disappearance of his crew at a time when he himself could not leave the boat, and in need of some information he had spotted Andy. Ignorant of Andy's affliction he had bellowed at him as he would have bellowed at any other boy who looked capable of delivering a message. Andy went to the edge of the pier.

"Away an' tell Bobbie I'm wantin' him down here!" he commanded. "You know Bobbie? The little fellow with the red hair?"

Andy nodded.

"Aye, then get him for me. Quick as you can, boy."

Gaymal children accepted that on the pier they were commanded to do things—never requested—and Andy ran to find Bobbie, but when the man saw it was the *Silver Crest* Andy was pointing to he turned away.

"I know fine what he wants me for," he told a crony, "and I'm not going. I'm supposed to be catching a train in half an hour and if Jake once gets a hold of me I might just as well wave it goodbye."

Andy returned to the *Silver Crest*.

"Well, did you find him?" Jake asked.

Andy nodded.

"Is he comin', then?"

Andy shook his head.

"Why isn't he comin'?"

Andy stared at Jake helplessly.

"What's wrong with you, boy? Have I got to dig

for every bit of an answer from you like I'd dig flesh from a limpet? What did he say?" Jake was becoming more exacerbated. "Are you wantin' a penny before you'll tell me what he said? Is that it?" Jake, used to the money-conscious Gaymal children, dug into his pocket and tossed a shilling onto the pier. Andy looked at the coin but made no attempt to pick it up.

"What in the hell's the matter with you?" Jake demanded. "Is it deaf, daft or dumb you are?"

Andy turned and ran quickly from his contempt. Jake climbed onto the pier hoping to spot another likely messenger, and the first two things he saw were the shilling he had thrown and the sketch Andy had been making of the *Silver Crest*. Jake pocketed the shilling, and picking up the paper he studied the drawing. It was nice, he thought. Fancy a stupid kid like that being able to draw as well as this. He turned the paper over and saw Andy's painstaking printing. " 'Dear Dad,' " he read. " 'This is the boat I like best in the harbor. She is called *Silver Crest* and I think she is beautiful.' " Jake wished he had not been so rough with the boy, and going back aboard, he placed the paper carefully between the leaves of a magazine in the wheelhouse thinking that the next time he saw Andy he would return it to him and at the same time tell him how good it was.

It was three weeks later when one of the crew came across the drawing and commented on it.

"Ach, I put it in there to give back to some kid that was on the pier doing it. I sent him to get Bobbie for me that day you lot skinned off ashore.

The kid came back without Bobbie and with not a word as to why." Jake's voice was scornful. "Proper little gaper he was, just standin' there an' sayin' nothin'. I shouted at him he must be dumb or somethin'."

"Did he have a dog with him? The one that used to belong to Joe?" asked one of the crew.

"Aye, I believe he did," Jake admitted.

"Aye, then right enough he is dumb," said the man, and turned away from his skipper's stricken face.

Later Jake learned from the crew the reason for Andy's arrival in Gaymal; learned too how he and the Spuddy had chummed up together and how the boy looked after the dog even though he was not allowed to have him anywhere near the house. The story touched Jake and as he thought it over he decided to try to make friends with the boy. To see if he could make some recompense for the hurt he had so unwittingly inflicted. Back in the wheelhouse he examined the drawing once more.

"I'll need to try an' get hold of the young fellow an' give him back his picture," he told the man at the wheel. "But God knows when I'll manage it, seein' he never comes near the boat since the day I turned on him."

chapter **11**

THE opportunity came when they limped back
into port with the seized engine, and Andy,
curiosity overcoming caution, was waiting on the
edge of the pier with the Spuddy, anxious to find
out what was wrong. When the crew had gone off
to the bar and the engineer was about to leave,
Andy started to move away. Jake's voice hailed him
and Andy looked back to where the skipper was
standing but he did not pause until he saw Jake
was holding out a paper. Reluctantly he turned and
went slowly up to him.

"Did you do this?" Jake asked as gently as he
could, and when Andy replied with a faint nod he

said, "It's good. I like it." He turned the paper over. "I read this too," he confessed. "Is it true you think this is the nicest boat in the harbor?" Andy released a nervous smile. "Aye, I think so too, boy," Jake admitted, looking proudly along the length of the *Silver Crest*. "I think so too," he repeated, and Andy heard the pride in his voice. "Are you comin' aboard?" he invited. Andy's expression was eloquent. "Come on, then, an' take a look over her."

Eagerly Andy climbed aboard followed by the Spuddy.

"Hey!" Jake objected. "I didn't invite that dog as well. Away you go!" The Spuddy looked questioningly at Andy before obeying the command. The next moment Andy was also ashore and standing beside the dog.

"What's all this?" Jake asked. "I thought you were keen to see over her." Andy put his hand on the Spuddy's head. "Okay, Okay," Jake yielded. "He may as well come too." Andy and the dog jumped back aboard and followed Jake enthusiastically into the wheelhouse, down into the hold, through to the engine room and finally into the fo'c'sle, where Jake put on the kettle.

"You get mugs an' rolls an' butter an' jam out of there," he instructed, pointing to a locker. "I daresay you won't say no to a bite to eat."

Andy did as he was told. He had never before eaten any sort of meal aboard a boat, and when Jake had made the tea and they sat on the lockers to eat and drink while the boat swayed to the tide Andy was blissfully happy. He had got over his fear of Jake and Jake was glad of having to entertain the boy and so shorten the hours he would otherwise have had to spend brooding over his misfortunes. All the same he was finding conversation solely by means of questions difficult to sustain and for much of the time they ate in silence. Jake noticed Andy giving the Spuddy a piece of every roll he took for himself, and recalling what the crew had told him about the dog being a stray that Andy had befriended and that he was not allowed to take home to his aunt's house, he wondered how much the boy fretted at having to leave the Spuddy at night.

"Does the Spuddy sleep in your room at home?" he probed.

Andy shook his head.

"In the kitchen? No? In the house at all? No? In a kennel outside, then?" Andy continued to shake his head. "Hasn't he got a place to sleep, then?" Jake saw Andy's eyes widen as if straining back the tears and he turned to fill the stove, making a clatter with the iron lid and the poker while wishing he hadn't asked questions to which he already knew the answers. But his only desire was to help the boy if he could.

Andy covered his eyes, anguished by the reminder of his problems. He tried pressing his hands very hard into his eyes but the tears seeped through. Jake saw them, and sitting down on the locker close to the boy, spoke without looking directly at him.

"I suppose you'd miss the Spuddy too much if I suggested he could be a sea dog?" he said.

Mystified, Andy looked up.

"Here on *Silver Crest*," Jake explained. "Why not? Lots of dogs go on boats," he went on. "An' there's folks say once a dog gets used to the sea he never wants to come ashore. Not to live, anyway."

Andy listened half dismayed and only half believing that Jake was serious. His eyes questioned, Why?

"He'd have a good berth with me an' the crew," Jake confided. "They're not hard, the men, an' there's always plenty of gash food aboard. An' there'd be a cozy bunk for him down here with us in the fo'c'sle. But"—Jake gave Andy a doubtful glance—"maybe you wouldn't like to be parted from him so much."

Andy stared steadfastly at Jake for some moments. He was grateful to him but he couldn't be parted from the Spuddy now. They needed each other too much.

"You'd see plenty of him at weekends," comforted Jake. But Andy could only think of the blank days of the week without the Spuddy for his companion. His heart plummeted as he thought how lonely life would be without him. Then he remembered about school and how he would be unable to see the Spuddy all day. He didn't know what to do. The village regarded the Spuddy as a stray. If Andy was at school and unable to look after him and if his bed at the boatyard was no longer available, what was going to happen? His only alternative was the cave, but that was so wet and cold that it just wouldn't do in the winter.

"How old are you?" Jake asked.

Andy held up nine fingers.

"That's a pity. I was going to say maybe you could join the crew too and you wouldn't have to be parted from the dog, but you're a mite young for that yet." Jake thought, If I get the chance and my son wants a dog, any sort of a dog, he shall have it sooner than I'll see him suffer like this lad's suffering. Aloud he said, "If you fancied comin' out fishin' with us you could come whenever you liked."

Andy smiled wanly. He knew what he ought to do but he could not bring himself to do it. He stood up, and nodding his thanks to Jake, started up the ladder from the fo'c'sle.

"Think on what I've said, now," Jake called after him.

Andy did think on it and after meeting Uncle Ben, who reminded him that the Spuddy could no longer sleep down at the boathouse, the boy and the dog once again made for the moors. The preceding autumn had lingered late and winter had followed its example. It was still bitterly cold with a biting wind that seared Andy's cheeks and filled his eyes with icy tears. When they reached the cave Andy slumped down beside it. This was no place for a dog in such weather. The rock roof was dripping wet and the wind had scattered the bedding. He stared straight ahead dejectedly, and the Spuddy, coming to lick his face, continued licking at the salty tears. Impatiently Andy pushed him away and then instantly regretting his action he pulled the dog close to him and buried his face in the rough coat. When he got up he knew what he must do. He gestured to the Spuddy to follow him.

They went first to the boatyard where Andy saw that already the Spuddy's bed had been cleared away to make room for lengths of timber. The Spuddy sniffed around them, looking every now and then at Andy as if asking where he was going to sleep. Andy sought out Uncle Ben and looked at him inquiringly while pointing at the Spuddy, but Uncle Ben could only shake his head. Out of a cupboard he took the dog's bowl and handed it to Andy. Andy and the Spuddy went purposefully down to the harbor.

Jake was still aboard the *Silver Crest*. He heard the thud of feet on the deck and opened the fo'c'sle hatch.

"Come on down, boy," he invited.

Obediently Andy, followed by the Spuddy, went down into the fo'c'sle. Swallowing hard, Andy reached out, and taking Jake's hand, placed it on the Spuddy's head. At the same time he held out the bowl.

Jake understood. When he spoke his voice was even gruffer than usual. "I'll look after him for you, boy," he promised. "And I'll not let him forget you."

Andy knelt down and put his arms around the Spuddy's neck.

"You'll want to see where he's goin' to sleep," Jake said. There were eight bunks in the fo'c'sle of the *Silver Crest* and Jake cleared out the lower of two which were obviously not used as sleeping accommodation for the crew. He extricated a couple of spare blankets from a locker and stuffed them into the bunk.

"That's your bunk, mate," he said to the Spuddy. The Spuddy only looked at him.

"You'd best tell him to get into it," Jake said, and Andy "told" the Spuddy in the special sign language the dog now understood so well. Reluctantly the Spuddy got into the bunk. Still more reluctantly he lay down. Gently Andy stroked him, and the fo'c'sle was quiet except for the slapping of the water against the boat.

"Aye, aye," said Jake awkwardly. "Likely he'll miss you but with time I daresay he'll settle down."

Andy showed the Spuddy his bowl and then placed it on the deck beside the bunk. Until now the dog had accepted that wherever Andy had placed his bowl, there was his home, and when he saw what Andy had just done he looked at him with the little wrinkle between his eyes that the boy knew was incredulity. Biting his lips hard, Andy turned away and went quickly up the fo'c'sle steps. The Spuddy jumped out of the bunk intent on following him but Jake held onto his collar. The dog struggled against Jake's restraint until Andy turned and made a repressive gesture. When Andy reached the deck Jake too climbed the steps and stood in the hatch, blocking the exit. The imprisoned Spuddy barked—a single sharp bark of protest.

"See you Saturday," said Jake. "An' don't forget if your aunt an' uncle aren't against it you can come with us whenever you have a chance," he called as Andy leaped ashore. Andy nodded, and Jake, seeing his crumpled young face, wished there were more he could do to comfort the boy. He stood watching while Andy ran along the pier and disappeared into the gathering dusk without once stopping to look behind him.

chapter **12**

BACK in the fo'c'sle the Spuddy and Jake assessed each other for a few moments, Jake sitting perfectly still on the locker and slouching across the table; the Spuddy sitting just as still but with his chin raised arrogantly. Then the dog, having realized from Andy's gestures that these were his new quarters, began to investigate the fo'c'sle thoroughly. After having stayed at Andy's bidding in the cave on the moors and then in the shed at the boatyard he knew now that he could trust the boy not to desert him. And after having for so long mingled with the fishermen he knew instinctively he could trust Jake. All he had to do was to go and settle himself down until the morning, when this man would open up the hatch and let him out to go and find Andy. He went to the bunk Andy had shown him and sat down beside it. Jake stood up and came over to him.

"That's your bunk, mate," he told the dog again. "An' remember, on a boat a man's bunk is a man's bunk—he swops with nobody an' nobody swops with him." He snapped his fingers over the bunk and obediently the Spuddy jumped in and crouched down. "Right," Jake resumed. "There's three things you have to learn aboard this boat an' you'll have to learn them pretty quick because nobody's goin' to have time to teach you. Are you listenin'?" The Spuddy's ears pricked intelligently and he cocked his head on one side. "The first is," Jake explained, "this is your home from now on until your pal can find you a better one. The second is, I'm your skipper from now on, an' the third is, like I've told you, this is your bed from now on."

The Spuddy, discerning the note of companionship in Jake's voice, thumped his tail once against the blankets, and the expression in his eyes as he watched Jake was one of perfect comprehension. Turning around in his bed, he settled down stiffly at first, but when he had seen Jake get into his own bunk he stood up, nuzzled the blankets into position and with a grunt settled down to sleep.

When the bar closed, the crew returned to the *Silver Crest*. "What's he doin' aboard?" they asked, seeing the Spuddy.

"Ship's dog," replied Jake laconically.

"Where's his kid, then?" asked the youngest crewman, recognizing the dog, and when Jake gave a brief explanation they murmured small pretended grumbles about having the dog aboard and said they hoped he would not be responsible for another run of bad luck.

"Not that one." Jake spoke with conviction. "There's somethin' about that dog that makes me think he's goin' to be our mascot. You just wait and see."

It was two o'clock in the morning before the engine was repaired satisfactorily and the *Silver Crest* was ready for sea. Until they were well out of port the skipper ordered that the Spuddy should be shut below deck, but once Jake thought it was safe he went down to the fo'c'sle, and threading a length of rope through the Spuddy's collar, took him up on deck. The night was dark and although the Spuddy had never before been to sea he knew the sound and smell of it so well he was not afraid when Jake led him along the deck to the wheelhouse. There, Jake shut the door and sat down, his hands on the wheel, his eyes fixed on the bow of his boat as it cleaved through the heaving sea.

"You may as well be here with me, boy," he told the Spuddy. "You an' me, we've got to get used to each other's company an' I reckon this is a good way to do it."

So the Spuddy stayed with Jake in the wheelhouse until it was time for Jake to be relieved, when they both returned to the fo'c'sle and their individual bunks. When daylight came and the Spuddy was allowed on deck without a rope he was worried because they were so far from land, and he roamed up and down from bow to stern and into the fish hold, hoping he might find Andy. When he was tired of roaming the deck he went back to his bunk and lay listening to the sound of the crew's voices as they ate and talked, and to the sound of their snores as they slept.

That night *Silver Crest* ran into an enormous shoal of herring, so that they came back to port gunwale deep with their load. The crew were jubilant, knowing that their run of ill luck had ended.

"Didn't I tell you he'd be our mascot?" Jake reminded them. And, their mascot the Spuddy came to be regarded. The following night they again ran into a large shoal and the next night again.

"He's worth his weight in steak every week," asserted the cook, as if daring any of them to question the sudden increase in the butcher's bill.

By the time Saturday morning came the Spuddy was just beginning to get used to his life as a ship's dog, to his warm bunk, to the good wholesome food plus the tidbits provided by the grateful crew; but when the boat tied up at the pier and he saw Andy waiting for him, he bounded ashore to greet him so ecstatically that had not Andy moved well back from the edge the two of them would undoubtedly have rolled into the water.

"I'll leave his dinner for him," called the cook as the boy and the dog raced off up the pier. Jake watched them go. "I hope he brings him back," said the cook. "We don't want our luck to run out."

"He'll be back," Jake assured him.

Andy felt a slight twinge of resentment when the cook had said he would leave the Spuddy's dinner. He was sure it was understood between him and Jake that except for his bunk aboard the *Silver Crest* the Spuddy was to be his alone at weekends, to care for as hitherto, and the cook's words seemed to imply that he thought Andy might neglect to feed the dog, whereas Andy had come with a haversack stuffed full of food both for the Spuddy and for himself. Aunt Sarah, now that she knew there was little likelihood of the dog's hanging around the house and annoying the new neighbors, had willingly set aside a "Spuddy pan" in which she not only boiled up house scraps but also added rough pieces of meat bought cheaply from the butcher, so that when Saturday came there was a big basinful of food ready for Andy to take to his friend. In addition, Andy, realizing that it was going to be awkward if he had to carry a feeding bowl to and from the *Silver Crest* each weekend, had bought him a new one so that the Spuddy would be as well catered for ashore as he was at sea.

It was a damp day, chafed by a gusty wind but with a hint of sun beyond the lowering clouds; a day when the moors echoed with muted gull cries and the burns, swollen after a night of rain, foamed peaty brown over the tumbled rocks. Andy plodded on, disturbing flocks of black-faced sheep

and wild goats and shaggy hill ponies who
watched suspiciously as he and the Spuddy climbed
toward a sheltered corrie which overlooked a great
chasm of fallen stone. Reaching it, he lay flat on
his stomach and the Spuddy lay quietly beside him.
Andy loved to come to the chasm not only because
of the tales Uncle Ben told of its being haunted
but because he liked to be awed by its sheer size
and desolation, and because if he lay quite still he
was sometimes lucky enough to catch a glimpse of
one of the elusive hill foxes that had their earths
among the chaos of tumbled stone that formed the
chasm's floor, or perhaps see one of the equally
elusive golden eagles launch itself from its perch
on a crevice of the sheer rock face.

The Spuddy sat up, and giving a faint whine,
put a paw on Andy's back. Andy knew without
looking at his watch that the Spuddy had decided
it was time for his dinner. As he tipped the boiled
meat scraps into the new bowl he wondered when
the Spuddy was fed aboard the *Silver Crest*. Fishermen could hardly he expected to abide by regular feeding times for a dog when they had little
chance of eating regularly themselves. Mealtimes
at sea, Andy knew, varied with the weather, the
herring shoals and the degree of exhaustion of the
crews.

The day passed quickly, and when it was time to
return, Andy and the Spuddy went aboard the
Silver Crest. The two were used to evening part-
ings and now the Spuddy quickly accepted that he
must stay aboard the boat while Andy went home.
With his two front paws resting on the sternpost

he watched until Andy was out of sight and then he slid under the half-open hatch, jumped down into the fo'c'sle and stretched himself out on his bunk. The following morning when Andy came down to the quiet Sunday morning harbor where the massed boats lay at rest and the strangely silent gulls were ranged along the roofs as stiffly as a church congregation he saw that the Spuddy was waiting for him, standing in exactly the same position with his two front paws on the sternpost and watching and listening as if he had been there all night.

As usual they made for the moors, the bulging haversack on Andy's back. Again in the evening, though earlier because it was Sunday and Andy had to accompany his Uncle Ben and Aunt Sarah to church, he saw the Spuddy back to the *Silver Crest*. But tonight the parting was more prolonged because Andy knew it would be another week before the Spuddy and he could be together again.

chapter 13

LONG before dawn, skipper Jake and the crew came aboard and soon the Spuddy heard the approach of other crews, and the harbor began to fill with the sound of throbbing boat engines; of voices shouting greetings, warnings, reminders and relieved "okays," as one by one the boats nudged their way out of the crowded harbor toward the open sea. The Spuddy looked out through the open hatch, and realizing they were leaving the land behind and there would be no Andy, returned disconsolately to his bunk and slept until the crew came down for their breakfast.

As a member of the crew of the *Silver Crest*

during the week and as Andy's faithful companion at weekends, the Spuddy began to know a contentment he had never before experienced and he did his best to show his appreciation. On the boat, when he saw the catches of herring coming aboard, the obvious excitement of the men affected him and he raced from stem to stern, from stern to stem, careful to keep out of everyone's way yet making sure he was sharing in the activity. Before long he was so anxious to help that he would grab at the net ropes when the men were hauling, and bracing himself, would pull with every ounce of muscle in his body.

"By God, we've got a dog and a half," the crew complimented one another, and Jake, watching from the wheelhouse, would whistle the Spuddy to come for an approbatory fussing and would remind himself that he must tell Andy about the Spuddy's latest achievement.

One night after a succession of good catches the *Silver Crest* appeared to have lost the shoals, and while they searched the seas in vain, the Spuddy spent his time running restlessly around the deck or else sitting wistfully in the bow staring into the night-black water. He was repeating this performance when Jake in the wheelhouse was surprised to hear him start to bark excitedly. It was the first time since he had been to sea with them that the Spuddy had been heard to bark, and Jake was puzzled. He was even more puzzled when, a few moments later, the dog came aft and began scratching impatiently at the wheelhouse door. Having grown fond of the Spuddy's company, Jake kicked open the door and waited for the dog to join him, but instead the Spuddy only pawed at him and whined.

"What is it, boy?" Jake asked. But the dog ran back to stand with his two front feet on the bow while he peered down into the water and his tail wagged ceaselessly. Jake eased the throttle and immediately a head appeared at the fo'c'sle hatch. "See what's botherin' him!" Jake shouted.

The youngest member of the crew came aft, pulling on an oilskin. "What's wrong, Skipper?"

"See what's botherin' the Spuddy," Jake repeated. "He's behavin' kind of queer, as if he can see or hear somethin'." The man went forward, and as he reached the bow the Spuddy's tail began to thrash even more vigorously and again he started to bark. The young man knelt down beside him, concentrating his attention on the sea. The cook came aft to join Jake.

"What's excitin' the dog?" the cook asked.

"Damned if I know," admitted Jake, and added uncertainly, "You'd think he must be hearin' or seein' somethin' the way he's actin'."

The man in the bow stood up, and turning gave a wide negative sweep of his arms.

"He can't see anythin' seemingly," said the cook.

Shouting to the Spuddy to be quiet, Jake throttled the engine down to a murmur, and handing over the wheel to the cook with the instruction to steer in a wide circle, he went out on deck and listened and looked intently. A minute later he was back in the wheelhouse.

"Go an' tell them to stand by to shoot the nets,"

he snapped. "It's my belief that dog's tryin' to tell us there's herrin'."

Flashing him an incredulous glance, the cook rushed forward to pass the command. An hour later they were gloatingly hauling in their loaded nets while the Spuddy looked on with smug triumph. Afterward down in the fo'c'sle the crew looked at one another in amazement and asked, "How did he do it, d'you reckon? By smell or by sight or by hearin'?"

"It's enough that he did it," the oldest crew member declared. "What we must wait an' see now is, can he do it again?"

The Spuddy not only did it again and again but he became such a reliable herring spotter that if he showed no interest in the area they were searching for fish, they knew there was little likelihood of finding any there. In Gaymal when the stories got around, the Spuddy, instead of being regarded as a stray, became a star, and though there were some fishermen who at first refused to believe in the dog's ability to detect the presence of herring, the *Silver Crest*'s consistently good catches were irrefutable evidence of his powers, and it was not long before skipper Jake was pointing out to his crew how even the most skeptical of the fishermen tended when at sea to keep the *Silver Crest* close company in the hope of sharing the Spuddy's largesse.

Andy was thrilled when he heard of the Spuddy's faculty for herring spotting. He was thrilled too by the pride in Jake's voice when he told him. At the time they had all three been down

in the fo'c'sle of the *Silver Crest*, where, to Andy's
delight, it had become more or less a habit for
them to meet on Saturday afternoons when he
and the Spuddy had returned from their walk.
While Jake talked of boats and fishing and of the
strange things that sometimes came up in their
nets they would sit beside the stove drinking the
skipper's peculiar brew of strong black tea sweet-
ened with condensed milk. Even the Spuddy now
drank the tea when it was poured into his bowl,
and Andy wondered if the dog really liked such a
potion, or if, like himself, he drank it only because
he would not have risked hurting Jake's feelings by
refusing it.

"Aye," Jake had said, rubbing the Spuddy's head
fondly. "It was the best thing you ever did for me,
letting me take your dog aboard." And Andy, who
was not unaware of Jake's drinking bouts and of
his loneliness, looked down at the strong hand resting on the Spuddy's head and at the dog's eyes
regarding his skipper, and at that moment his last
trace of resentment at having to share the Spuddy
vanished.

chapter **14**

AS the months went by the Spuddy was acknowl-
edged by everyone to have become a cher-
ished and indispensable member of the crew of the
Silver Crest. In addition to herring spotting he had
resumed his war with the gulls, racing along the
deck and leaping with snapping jaws at any gull
who dared to swoop too low, and protecting the
catch at unloading time as fiercely as he had at one
time protected the fish for which Joe was responsible. He took all his self-imposed duties seriously
and at weekends when he was left in charge of
the boat at night he guarded it like a sentry, so
that crews from other boats moored alongside com-

plained that, though he allowed them to cross his deck in daylight, when returning drunk at night they had to "give the password like bloody soldiers before he'd let you cross."

On board he could be trusted to keep out of the way of the crew's feet when they were busy on deck, and except for falling overboard one pitch-black night into a heaving sea while the skipper and crew were all too busy hauling to notice his disappearance, he did nothing that would cause them concern. That night the Spuddy had been really frightened, but sensibly he had fought the sea to swim around the boat to the side where the nets were being hauled, and gripping the footrope of the net with teeth and legs, he clung on. It was not until the incredulous crew saw him being hauled in with the net that they realized he must have fallen overboard and how near they must have been to losing him. Jake's fear had erupted into a flash of anger and he swore at the Spuddy vehemently, ordering him down to the fo'c'sle, but afterward when things had quietened down Jake laughed to himself, thinking he had never seen the dignified Spuddy look so utterly ridiculous and dejected as he had when he was being hauled aboard along with a load of herring. Jake called the dog back to the wheelhouse to give him a teasing and patting, but following that night he always made sure the Spuddy was shut safely in the fo'c'sle when they were actually hauling and he never dared tell Andy of the incident.

There was no doubt, the *Silver Crest* became a happier boat after the Spuddy had become its mascot. The crew liked him to be there because it made the boat seem more homely. Jake was glad of his companionship in the wheelhouse during the long hours on deck, glad too of the dog's apparent need of him. It was good to be needed, Jake mused, remembering with lacerating bitterness his last meeting with his wife. Resolving to make a final attempt to persuade Jeannie that, particularly now they had a child, her rightful place was in the home he had provided for her, he had tied up the *Silver Crest*, given his crew a week's holiday and gone to visit her at the home of her parents.

Jeannie had seemed pleased enough to see him but his son, now a toddler, had to be coaxed into recognizing him, and Jake was pained to see that he preferred the company of the doting grandfather to his own. When, toward the end of the week, he broached the subject of her return, Jeannie had been at first evasive and then impatient. Couldn't he see for himself her mother was getting frail and needed to be looked after? she had demanded sharply, and at the same time had wanted to know how her father was expected to manage the work of the croft without the help of his daughter. Jake had tried to convince her of his own need of her and of his longing for his son, but though she had promised to come back soon and spend more time with him he knew from her manner that the promise was an empty one. She would just find more urgent excuses for staying away, though Jake knew she would never leave him in the accepted sense. An island girl never "left" her husband; she only retreated from him slowly but inexorably to the home of her parents, where she would accept continued maintenance from her husband in return for being apathetically available should he wish to visit her at any time.

Meantime Jake's thwarted affections were given to the Spuddy, whose own feelings for his skipper had deepened from trust to affection and finally into much the same devotion as he felt for Andy. There was a difference, though. Whereas Andy was his beloved friend and companion, because the boy was young the Spuddy regarded him as a charge to be protected. But Jake with his quiet strength fulfilled the strong-minded Spuddy's need for a master who would protect him.

chapter **15**

IT was about three months after the Spuddy had
joined the crew that Andy at last achieved his
ambition to go to sea in the *Silver Crest*. The forecast of a spell of settled weather happening to
coincide with a school holiday prompted Jake to
suggest that it would be a good chance for Andy
to have his first fishing trip, and seeing the boy's
undoubted pleasure at the prospect, Jake himself
had approached Uncle Ben, who in turn had put
the proposal to Aunt Sarah. After making a few
fussy provisos Aunt Sarah had given her permis-
sion. Since it was to be a midnight start it was
decided to Andy's great joy that instead of his

staying up long past his usual bedtime or going early to bed and having to get up again within a few hours, he would go down to the *Silver Crest* at his usual bedtime and sleep aboard. So it was that one tranquil Sunday evening when the moored boats lay black against a sea that was stippled with starlight Andy found himself boarding the *Silver Crest* to be greeted by a surprised and delighted Spuddy, who, having as usual spent the day with Andy and having as usual returned to the boat in the late afternoon, had not expected to see him again until after another week at sea. Together they went below, and Andy had only just finished taking off his oilskins when he heard someone coming aboard. The hatch was pushed back and skipper Jake came down into the fo'c'sle.

"Welcome aboard," he greeted Andy, and in reply to the boy's questioning look, explained "Aye, I'm kippin' aboard myself tonight." Andy was disappointed. He had hoped to pretend he and the Spuddy were the skipper and mate of the *Silver Crest* for a few hours and he wondered if Jake's presence was one of Aunt Sarah's provisos of which he had not been told.

"Your bunk's the one above the Spuddy's," Jake told him. "You'll find blankets in the locker there." He patted the Spuddy roughly. "I'll take a bet this fellow was mighty pleased to see you back?" The Spuddy looked from man to boy and panted happily.

Andy got blankets from the locker and Jake showed him how to line his bunk with them so that he would be snug during the night. Jake also showed him how to light the galley stove, and when the kettle had boiled and they had made tea they sat drinking it in the quiet of the cabin.

"Now, boy, it's kippin' time," said Jake, standing up. Andy took Jake's empty cup and his own half empty one and washed them at the galley sink. "That's what I like to see," Jake approved. "Tidiness aboard a boat. On deck an' below, a boat's a better place for being tidy." Taking off his boots and his jacket he slid into his bunk, realizing as he did so it was the first Sunday night for months that he had gone to bed sober. "Goodnight!" he grunted, and pulled the blankets up over his face. Andy saw that the Spuddy had already settled himself down for the night and he began taking off his own boots. Climbing into his bunk he inserted himself between the folds of blanket and lay down. The bunk fitted him like a coffin, leaving no room for restlessness, and he lay savoring the atmosphere of the man's world which now enclosed him, exulting in the sway of the boat and the trilling of the sea against the planking. He told himself he did not want to sleep but only to close his eyes against the glow of the lamp while he anticipated the excitement that morning would bring.

He was shot into wakefulness by the thud of seaboots on the deck above his head and he rolled out of his bunk as the fo'c'sle hatch was slammed back and one by one the crew came down. They greeted him morosely, still bemused with their weekend excesses, and Andy stood beside his bunk watching them as they stowed their gear. They woke Jake and went back on deck, and soon after-

ward Andy heard the engine clang to life and settle
to a steady throbbing. He pulled on his boots and
stood peering out of the hatch, fearing he might
be accused of getting in the way if he ventured up
on deck. In the light from the masthead he
watched the mooring ropes being taken aboard
and coiled neatly on the deck. He felt the *Silver
Crest* push away from the pier and heard the
water splashing against her stem. Jake stayed in
the wheelhouse while the men came back to the
fo'c'sle where the kettle was already steaming on
the stove, and while the cook brewed tea the crew
lit cigarettes and pipes. The fo'c'sle quickly became
stuffy and thick with smoke and Andy was full of
yawns.

"Why don't you get back to your bunk like your
pal there?" asked the cook, indicating the Spuddy,
who was still stretched out luxuriously while keeping just half an eye on the activity. "When we start
fishin' there'll be plenty of time for you to come
up on deck an' watch us."

Andy went back to his bunk, but finding himself too tense to sleep he got up again, and pulling
on his boots and oilskins, prepared to go and join
Jake. After the stuffiness of the fo'c'sle, the cold, as
he stepped on deck, smote him sharply, almost
making him gasp. The Spuddy moved surely beside
him but Andy found his feet were unsteady and
he was glad to hold onto the mast and the coam-
ings of the hatches as he scrambled his way to the
wheelhouse. The sea was by no means rough, but
to Andy, who was used only to walking the decks
of moored boats, the *Silver Crest* seemed to have

come alive and to be behaving in a strangely willful manner. Jake opened the door of the wheelhouse.

"Not got your sea legs yet," he observed. Andy smiled wryly. "Never mind, it won't take you too long an' you're best to be practicin' in the dark to begin with." He made room for Andy on the seat beside him. "Even the Spuddy took a while to get used to it an' he's got twice as many legs as you to keep him stable," he added.

Andy stared out through the window of the wheelhouse and as his eyes accustomed themselves to the darkness he began to pick out the masthead lights of other boats bound for the same fishing grounds. Jake looked down at him.

"Enjoying yourself so far?" he asked. Andy smiled. "Like to take the wheel for a bit?" he invited, and Andy, hardly able to believe his ears, took over the steering of the *Silver Crest* while Jake rolled and lit a cigarette. The cook appeared bringing steaming mugs of tea and thick wads of bread spread with butter and jam. Jake took the wheel again while Andy ate.

"We shouldn't be too long before we find somethin'," he said after they had been steaming for about two hours. "There was herring here last week, so as likely as not they'll be here yet." As he spoke he was throttling down the engine. The Spuddy shook himself into alertness as Jake opened the wheelhouse door. "He knows fine what's happenin' now," Jake explained to Andy, "an' if he doesn't show any interest we'll not bother to shoot our nets."

But the Spuddy did show interest. Going to the forepeak of the boat he stood looking down into the water, and to Andy it seemed that he was not only looking but that he was listening intently. The *Silver Crest* speared on, and as the crew began to come up on deck, fastening their oilskins and pulling on their sou'westers, there was a pale promise of dawn touching the horizon. Suddenly the Spuddy's tail began to wag and he started to bark.

"Okay, now!" shouted Jake to Andy. "You an' the Spuddy get below where you'll be safe." But seeing Andy's disappointed expression he added, "All right, you can stick your head out of the hatch there an' watch, but see that you keep that dog down below." Andy did as he was told.

The engine slowed. "Standby!" Jake yelled, and then, minutes later, "Shoot!"

Andy stood in the hatchway, stunned by the spectacle of the great pile of nets emerging from the hold and streaming out over the side while one of the crew busily tied buoys onto the rope warp. There seemed to be miles and miles of net and he wondered whether they would ever get it all back aboard again.

"Okay," said Jake as the last of the nets went out. The engine was slowed until she was just ticking over, and the crew went below while the *Silver Crest* lay to waiting until Jake gave the order to return to the deck. "Haul!" commanded the skipper crisply.

If Andy had been impressed by the sight of the nets going out he was spellbound when they began to come in again. As the men strained at the ropes, heaving and hauling and shaking the nets, and the quivering stream of herring poured onto the deck and down into the fishhold, Andy could only gape with astonishment. What a story he would have to tell his father next time he wrote! He was still standing enthralled after the last of the nets were in and the crew had finished tidying the deck, and was startled by the sound of Jake's voice telling them to go and get their heads down for an hour. He looked at Andy.

"What about you, boy?" he asked. "You could do with trying to get a bit of sleep yourself." Andy shook his head. He had only just realized that dawn had spread itself over the sky and that a metal-bright sun was groping its way through a throng of morning clouds. He followed Jake into the wheelhouse, knowing he was far too excited to think of sleep, and anyway he was determined to be up on deck for the homeward journey. Determined that no part of this wonderful day should be wasted in sleeping.

The cook came aft with more tea and bread and jam, and while he drank and ate, Andy watched the sea, ruffled now by an early breeze and flecked by sunlight. He saw the bowspray threaded with rainbows and heard the gulls pleading for a taste of the catch. The Spuddy heard the gulls too and was quick to station himself on deck ready for the attack.

"They'll not come near," Jake assured Andy. "Not while he's here." He smiled grimly. "Watch those blackbacks now," he said, pointing to some gulls that were daring to hover around the *Silver*

Crest's masthead. "Just watch them. There's nothin' they'd like better than to best the Spuddy." Andy tried to watch them but his eyes would not focus. "See now," said Jake, as one of the blackbacks tried swooping low over the deck, but turning around to catch Andy's expected smile, Jake saw that he had fallen asleep, his head against a corner of the wheelhouse and a half-eaten slice of bread-and-jam still held in his hand.

chapter **16**

SUBSEQUENTLY Andy spent as much of his time as possible on the *Silver Crest,* but it was not until his next half-term holiday that he was again able to spend the night aboard, and that night Jake had cause to be grateful for the presence of both Andy and the Spuddy. They had sailed early on the Thursday morning, making for fishing grounds some hours steaming away; and though the weather forecast was far from good, Jake thought they might be lucky enough to haul a few cran of herring before they had to return. The sea was gray and restless, sending up great sheets of spray to break over the bow of the boat as she plowed into

it, and Andy was glad he had now got his sea legs
so that his body responded easily to the motion.
When they reached the fishing grounds they had
hardly shot their nets before the storm came with
unexpected force, making it necessary for them to
haul and run with their meager catch to the shelter
of the nearest harbor.

As was their custom when in port, Jake and the
crew repaired to the local bar, leaving Andy and
the Spuddy in charge of the boat. Andy, tired after
the early start and the buffeting of the storm, took
the Spuddy on only a short exploration of the
harbor before returning to the boat and seeking
his bunk, where he was soon fast asleep. The
Spuddy, however, always mistrustful of strange
harbors, elected to remain on deck where, crouched
down behind the wheelhouse, he could keep watch
while sheltered from the worst of the wind. Jake
was the first to return, and, sodden with whisky,
he was halfway down the slimy harbor steps when
the Spuddy, waiting eagerly on board to greet him,
saw him slip and fall into the water.

Even in the harbor the sea was tempestuous, and
Jake, who could not swim and who was encumbered
with oilskins and heavy thigh boots, would have
stood little chance of survival had he not managed to grasp one of the fenders. Immediately the
Spuddy started to prance around the deck, barking
frenziedly and waking Andy, who stumbled up
from the fo'c'sle to find out what was the matter.
The Spuddy showed him where Jake was still
clinging on, and Andy did the first thing that came

into his mind, which was to lie down flat on the
deck behind the gunwale and reach down a hand
for Jake to grasp. He found his reach too short, so
that as the boat reared and the water surged his
hand was tantalizingly a foot above the fender. He
tried heaving at the fender but he had not suffi-
cient strength to pull up the sodden fender plus
the weight of the man. He next half slid, half
crawled along the deck to find a rope that he
might drop to Jake, but even as he was searching,
the Spuddy had decided on his own course of
action. Still barking frenziedly and ignoring the
danger should he misjudge the distance, he leaped
from the deck of one heaving boat to another
until he had every crew aboard rolling out of their
bunks and coming up on deck to demand: "What
the hell's the matter with that bloody dog?"

Fortunately some of the crews realized instantly
from the Spuddy's behavior that something was
wrong, and rushing to follow him back to the
Silver Crest, they saw Andy's desperate struggles
to hold onto Jake. Within minutes Jake was safely
back in his bunk, wrapped in blankets and plied
with even more whisky to "kill the cold." When
the other crews had returned to their boats Andy
stoked up the fo'c'sle stove and made coffee. He
stirred condensed milk into hot water and poured
a liberal quantity into the Spuddy's bowl and
watched while the dog drank appreciatively. Then
he went to Jake's bunk, and pulling the blanket
away from his face, indicated the hot coffee questioningly.

Jake raised himself on an elbow. "No, no," he said. "Thanks, boy, all the same," he mumbled sheepishly.

The Spuddy, hearing his voice, came and reared up beside the bunk, and Jake, seeing him, put out a hand and roughly grasped a handful of the dog's shaggy coat. He looked at Andy.

"By God! You're a real pair of mates, you two," he said. "I would have been a goner if it hadn't been for you two."

Andy smiled and the Spuddy wagged his tail. Jake's hand loosened its grasp of the Spuddy as he lay back in his bunk. "Real mates," he repeated drowsily, and pulled the blankets up over his head.

The next morning the storm still raged and skipper and crew slept in. Andy saw to the stove, made his breakfast and took the Spuddy for a walk around the harbor. Returning, he met the bleary-eyed crew just coming ashore.

"We're away to have a look 'round the shops before we go," they told Andy. "Comin' with us?" Andy smiled and shook his head. He knew Jake would be alone and he was anxious to get back to the boat. Aboard the *Silver Crest* Jake was up and pouring himself a mug of tea.

"So you're back from your wanders," he greeted Andy, and tapping the teapot, asked, "Will you take a cup?" Andy got out his mug from the locker and also put out the Spuddy's bowl. Jake filled them both up. He pushed the tin of condensed milk toward Andy.

"Well, it was a bad do last night," he admitted with a shamefaced smile. "But I'm none the worse, thank God." He stirred the tinned milk into his own tea and into the Spuddy's bowl. Andy watched the skipper pour a dose of whisky into his cup, from which he took several quick gulps.

Noticing that Andy's eyes were still fixed on him, Jake wondered if he was expected to again express his appreciation of his rescue. His mind was fumbling for suitable words when Andy got up and went to his bunk. Jake watched him rummage beneath the mattress and saw him take out a well-stuffed folder. Moving toward Jake, Andy laid it diffidently on the table in front of him. Jake looked at Andy, then down at the folder and again at Andy quizzically. "D'you want me to open it?" he asked. Andy nodded, his eyes dark with excitement. Carefully Jake opened the folder, and as he saw the drawings something in the boy's attitude made him realize how honored he was. He felt a sudden stab of emotion at Andy's trust in him, and as he fingered through them he saw that there were many drawings of the *Silver Crest*.

"These are great," he said with clumsy admiration. Andy beamed at him. Jake looked up. "These are beautiful, Andy," he enthused.

Still beaming, Andy slid onto the bunk beside him and together they inspected the folder of drawings.

chapter 17

ANOTHER year passed during which Andy's father came home on leave three times, and so reassuring was his son's appearance that he was able to return to sea contented. Though he had kept Aunt Sarah informed of his divorce and his wife's subsequent remarriage and departure for Australia, he hadn't mentioned the subject to Andy, partly because he did not wish to mar their infrequent holidays together and partly because he hoped that avoidance of the subject might help Andy to forget more quickly.

At first Andy had wanted his father to tell him about his mother, but he came to accept his reluctance and asked no questions, although now that he could read and write there was nothing to prevent him from doing so. It was so long now and she had rejected him so completely that he did not wish to think about her. He was happy with things as they were. He had school, which so far he had not learned to dislike; he had an affectionate home with Uncle Ben and Aunt Sarah and he had the Spuddy and skipper Jake and the *Silver Crest*. His life was too full for brooding. He had become accepted by the crew of the *Silver Crest* as "ship's boy" and joined them whenever he was on holiday from school, but though Jake had invited him more than once, he had not been lucky enough to go on one of her longer trips lasting several days.

His first chance to go he had missed because of the flu; his second chance had come and gone when he was in bed with measles, and when the next school holidays came along they coincided with the annual laying up of the boats for "paint up." Andy began to doubt that he would ever be able to take part in a real fishing trip: one lasting long enough so that he would get to sleep aboard for more than one night and which would mean they were landing their catch at strange ports where he could go ashore with the crew and perhaps be mistaken for one of them instead of always being recognized as "Andy the Dummy."

The following year, when the spring holiday was approaching, Andy was elated to hear Jake say one Saturday morning: "I believe you're gettin' a holiday from school next week. We're aimin' to land at a different port so it'll be a kind of longish trip. See now you don't go takin' anythin' wrong with you that will keep you to your bed. I'll speak to your Uncle Ben about you comin' with us."

Andy's response was a broad smile which cut itself off as he remembered his father was due home on leave next week. But Andy was sure his father would understand. He wouldn't want him to miss his chance yet again, he told himself, and anyway since his father's leaves always lasted at least three weeks there would be plenty of time for them to be together when he returned from his trip.

The spring holiday came with unspringlike wet and cold and sleet, and when the *Silver Crest* speared out to sea at first light on Monday morning Andy was glad to be able to share the shelter of the wheelhouse with Jake and the Spuddy. The crew were suffering from sore heads and Jake was miserably aware of his own hangover and of the pain stabbing at his stomach. Hunched over the wheel he scowled at the tossing sea as he steered for the thick, gray horizon. The cook came aft, ducking his head against the spray and sleet.

"Are you goin' to get your head down, Skipper?" he asked, reaching for the wheel.

"Aye, I'll do that," replied Jake. "It's not much of a day, so how about makin' for that Rhuna place of yours; seein' you're always tellin' us how sheltered it is in this wind? We could maybe lie to in the bay for a whiley until we see what the weather's goin' to do. You can pilot us through the passage yourself."

"Aye, aye, Skipper," agreed the cook.

Jake spoke to Andy. "You'd best get some kip

yourself, boy, while you can," he instructed. "If we're fishin' tonight you'll not get a chance."

Obediently Andy went to his bunk, where he lay listening to the heavy thump of the boat into the seas; the scrunch of the waves and the smacking of spray on the deck. Thump, scrunch, smack; thump, scrunch, smack. The rhythm was like a cradlesong.

Andy woke to the noise of the chain rattling through the fairlead as the *Silver Crest* dropped anchor in Rhuna bay. He slid quickly out of his bunk and went on deck to stand shivering in the first bite of the wind. Rhuna bay, hugged by two arms of jagged land, was relatively quiet, though the waves were fussing and hissing around the black rocks and the wind in the boat's rigging had a high-pitched note of menace. Andy could see the low gray stone croft houses set close to the shore, and beyond them, where the land rose to meet the hills, he discerned drifts of brown and black cattle grazing on the tawny grass. Skipper Jake, who had been up on deck to supervise the anchoring, paused to glare at the livid sky above the plump gray clouds that sagged over the hill peaks before returning to the fo'c'sle, where, his face taut with pain, he threw himself into his bunk. Andy, aware of his own sea-appetite, joined the rest of the crew in a meal of bacon, eggs and sausages along with the usual hot, dark tea thickened with condensed milk and sipped from pint-size enameled mugs. Just as they were finishing the meal they heard a boat scrape alongside and the youngest crew member went up to investigate. He returned a few minutes later with two middle-aged men dressed in what Andy took to be their Sunday clothes. The cook was quick to recognize the men, and when they had exchanged a few sentences in Gaelic he translated. "They're sayin' there's a weddin' on here today. One of my relatives it's supposed to be, too."

There were questioning murmurs from the rest of the crew. "Aye, an' they're after askin' us over an' take a wee dram with them an' maybe have a crack an' wish the bride an' groom good luck." The cook's expression was eager. "How about it, boys? Just for an hour or two?"

It took only a short discussion to reveal that all the crew liked the idea of going ashore for an hour, and when they woke Jake to submit their plan to him he not only agreed but insisted they take Andy with them.

"You may as well take the Spuddy too, Andy," Jake said, dragging himself out of his bunk to see them go. "A run ashore won't do him any harm."

But surprisingly, when the time came for the Spuddy to jump into the dinghy, he refused to go. Even when Andy tried coaxing by patting the seat beside him and by pointing to the hills the Spuddy still did not yield. Andy noticed a slight quiver passing through the dog's body, and thinking he might be sick, he stood up in the dinghy intent on climbing back aboard so as to stay with him. The youngest crew member pulled him down, again.

"You can come to the party instead of goin' for a walk, Andy. You'll fairly enjoy yourself," he asserted. Andy still looked troubled, but by now the dinghy was pushing off.

The cook, who had also noticed the Spuddy quivering, called banteringly up to Jake, "Ach, I believe the dog's feelin' his age the same as the rest of us. The fishin' life's as hard on a dog as it is on a man. We all age quicker than we should."

Jake gave the Spuddy a pat. "Aye, we're all feelin' our age," he responded with a sardonic smile. He was glad to be left alone for a little while. An hour's quiet and Jake was confident he'd be himself again. The anchor was good; the sea was quiet enough in the bay, and even though the crew were ashore, Jake trusted them to keep an eye open for anything going amiss. He went back to his bunk to collapse in a stupor of pain. The Spuddy, having watched the dinghy reach the safety of the shore, followed his skipper to the fo'c'sle and stretched himself out in his own bunk.

Jake was roused by the Spuddy's sharp, insistent barking. He was out of his bunk in a second. "What the hell?" he asked himself, recognizing by the motion of the boat that something was wrong. "The bloody anchor's dragged," he muttered, consternated, and stumbled on deck to be met by a blinding blizzard that made him bend double as his eyes flinched shut.

Close at hand he could hear the noise of breakers muffled by the snow but still far too loud. God! She was almost ashore! He rushed to start the engine. Where in hell's name were the crew? Why hadn't they noticed the change in the weather, blast them! He'd trusted them, hadn't he? Fool that he was. Once the engine began to throb confidently his mind could grapple with the next prob-

lem. The anchor! Dismissing the possibility of trying to get it aboard himself he ran forward to cast
off the anchor chain. That was a loss the crew
could pay for, he thought grimly as he raced back
to the wheelhouse and put the engine in gear.

He tried to peer through the blizzard for a sign
of the dinghy bringing out the crew but the snow
was impenetrable, obliterating everything beyond
the outline of the boat. Cautiously Jake began to
dodge the *Silver Crest* toward the entrance of the
bay while cursing himself for being rash enough
to allow all the crew to go ashore at the same time;
for relying on the cook to pilot him through the
narrow Rhuna passage. Where was that bloody
cook? What was it he'd said to avoid? Remembered
snatches of fo'c'sle talk rushed confusedly through
his mind and Jake recalled with mounting panic
something about there being a couple of rocks,
submerged at high tide and well out beyond the
coast to the west of the island. Just where were the
rocks? And how far out must he steer to avoid
them?

He was shouting curses now; cursing himself,
the cook and the snow. How near was he coming to
the entrance of the bay? How soon could he risk
turning? Gradually he became aware of a sharp
lift to the sea and he heaved a sigh of relief, knowing that he must be approaching open water.
Resolving to turn westward rather than risk the
hazardous passage between Rhuna and the mainland, he headed the *Silver Crest* directly into the
seas, revving up the engine to combat the rapidly
worsening conditions. Despite the cold, his body

was running with sweat; his hands, even his arms, were shaking as he clutched the wheel, and he found himself no longer shouting curses but murmuring prayer after fervent prayer as the boat leaped and plunged.

The crash as she came down on the rocks flung Jake to the deck while the mast came smashing through the top of the wheelhouse. For a moment he lay stunned, blood welling from a great gash on the side of his head, and then he was desperately struggling to his feet to slam the engine into full astern. The propeller raced uselessly, and as the sea tumbled away he saw that the *Silver Crest* was caught amidships by two great fangs of rock that were holding her above the water like a priest holding up a sacrifice. Jake moaned. Why hadn't he gone out more before turning? How had he come to so badly misjudge his distance from the shore? The bloody snow! His stomach burned with pain and he clutched at it as he retched blood onto the deck.

Staggering forward, he clung on as another mountainous sea raced and reared to smash itself over the rocks and then all Jake was conscious of was the assault of the thundering water and the screams of his boat as she keeled over and the sea and the rocks began rending her apart.

Gasping, he lay on the tilting deck, his hands gripping the capping, while the realization that his boat was doomed soaked into his brain as pitilessly as the chill sea soaked into his weakening body. He glimpsed the rocks again spiking through the snarling water; grasping, greedy rocks. Jake's

breath came in sobbing coughs. They'd got his
boat and now they wanted him. Those rocks, they
wanted him all right. The thought hammered
itself repetitively into his brain and he thought
of his wife who didn't want him and of his infant
son who didn't need him.

Suddenly he remembered the Spuddy. Where
was he? Could he still be down in the fo'c'sle?
Gulping and gasping, Jake pulled himself along,
hanging onto the fallen mast only to find that the
seas were breaking through the fo'c'sle hatch. The
Spuddy must have got out, Jake reasoned. Was he
even now swimming for the shore? Jake hoped so,
but even as the hope entered his mind he saw the
Spuddy.

When the mast had fallen the dog must have
come up from the fo'c'sle and have been trying to
reach him in the wheelhouse, and he lay now, his
hindquarters pinned down by the wreckage. The
Spuddy's mouth was open and he might have been
howling, though Jake could hear nothing above
the savagery of the sea.

"All right, Spuddy!" he panted. Slithering and
clawing his way along the deck he at last managed
to insert his shoulder under the mast and heaved
with all his remaining strength. Weak as he was,
the effort was enough to release the Spuddy and
the next sea did the rest, washing the dog into the
water. Relieved, Jake saw that he could still swim.
The Spuddy might stand a chance of getting
ashore alive. A dog's chance. No more. In the next
instant he perceived the Spuddy was trying to turn
to swim back to him.

"No, Spuddy! No!" Jake's voice came out in a rasping shout. "Ashore, Spuddy! Ashore! Skipper's orders!" Through a thinning swirl of snow Jake thought he caught a glimpse of land. He retched again and slowly his hands released their grip of the boat.

chapter **18**

BACK in Rhuna the crew, caught up in the gaiety of the wedding, failed to notice the passing of time and the threatening storm. Even Andy was too entranced by the old fiddler's playing to give a thought about getting back to the Spuddy. He had seen the sky darken and a few snowflakes whirling about, but the house in which they were being entertained was tucked in behind the hill out of sight of the sea, so it was not until they judged the time had come for them to return to the boat and they had rounded the shoulder of the hill that they became aware of the full force of the blizzard. When they reached the shore they were concerned to find that the sea was breaking so viciously over the shingle it was impossible to launch the dinghy.

Andy could not hide his anxiety, but the crew, feeling guilty over their inattention to the weather, tried to reassure themselves that there was nothing to worry about. When the tide ebbed there'd be a chance to launch the dinghy, they consoled themselves. And this blizzard couldn't last long, surely: not coming down as thickly as it was.

They accepted the hospitality of a cottage near the shore where they drank tea and smoked and bit their fingernails and stared as though hypnotized at the snow-masked windows. From his corner beside the fire Andy watched, feeling their unspoken apprehension. It was almost dark before the blizzard ceased and the sea was calm enough for them to get out the dinghy, and by that time there was no *Silver Crest* in the bay.

"She must have started draggin' her anchor an' so he thought he'd best get out of it," suggested the youngest member of the crew.

"I daresay that's the way of it," agreed the cook.

"In that case he'll soon be back to pick us up," said the oldest, and they clustered around the dinghy, kicking at the shingle, stamping their cold feet; flapping their arms; smoking; muttering; exclaiming; and all the time staring out across the bay willing the lights of the *Silver Crest* to appear around the point. The wind died to a frosty calm and a full moon rose, polishing the dark rocks against the snowy collar of the bay, and still the men waited on the shore, refusing the proffered warmth of the cottage. When the dawn came and there was still no sign of the boat, the crew and some of the crofters walked out to the point to scan the sea. What they saw impaled on the jagged rocks sent some of them to summon help while others hurried to search the rocky shores.

When the sea had flung the Spuddy on the sandy inlet between the rocks on Rhuna's west coast, it was the top of the tide, and after dragging himself out of reach of the water he lay quite still. All through the night, oblivious of the thrashing surf, the cold and the pain of his crushed body, he waited for the peace he knew would not be long in coming. When dawn came, lifting his head as if for one last look, he saw lying just above the now calm water the body of his skipper. He tried to move, digging his paws into the sand, and laboriously, shuddering every now and then with pain, he dragged himself down until he was lying beside Jake. As he nuzzled under the cold hand that had given him so many rough caresses, his tail lifted and dropped once and his breath came out in a last long moan.

Man and dog were still lying together when the search party found them. Gently they moved the body of the Spuddy aside while they lifted Jake onto a makeshift stretcher and carried him away. When they had gone, Andy, accompanied by his father, who had been told on his arrival in Gaymal of the wreck and had hitched a lift on the first boat out to Rhuna, reached the place where the Spuddy lay. Andy's father let the boy go down to the shore alone, and as he watched he saw Andy bend down and tenderly rest his hand on the dog's wet body. He saw him go then to where the shattered bow of the *Silver Crest* lay where it had been washed ashore; saw him run his hand down the curving stem as he might have run it along the neck of a favorite horse; saw him return to the Spuddy and kneel beside him in the sand.

He turned away then so as not to witness his son's grief, and crouching behind a rock he looked up at the gulls as they circled low over the shore, listening to the laughterlike mutterings of a couple of blackbacks, the loud harsh screams of the herring gulls. Then, thinking he heard a human shout, he looked around him to see who might be coming. He stood up. The shout seemed to be coming from the direction of the shore, but he knew there was only Andy down there. Andy and a dead dog. He looked more intently. The shout was unmistakably coming from the shore.

"No! No! No!" it was saying over and over again, and as Andy, his son, was shaking his fists at the low swooping gulls his mouth was forming the word No! and the sound was without doubt coming from it.

He stood in dazed unbelief while he watched Andy pull some cord from his pocket, tie one end of it around a boulder and the other around the Spuddy's neck. He saw him drag the dog down and into the water, and fearful of what might happen, he started bounding down to the shore calling, "Andy! Andy!"

But Andy paid no attention. He knew he had to do this last service for his friend. He couldn't let the enemy gulls ravage the poor dead body that could no longer defend itself. He must get the Spuddy out to deep water—deep enough to be out of the way of the gulls and where the boulder would ensure that he would be carried out to sea by the next tide. As his father splashed through the water to his side Andy let go of the boulder and the Spuddy. He grasped the hand his father was holding out to him.

"Andy!" rejoiced his father as they waded ashore. "You spoke. Did you know?"

Andy's hand went to his throat. "No!" he said, but he was not answering his father's question, he was still shouting at the gulls.

"But you spoke again then. You really did," his father insisted.

"Yes," said Andy experimentally, and feeling the strange throbbing that had begun in his throat, he said "Yes" and "No," "Yes" and "No," over and over again as together he and his father climbed out of the bay and tramped back across the snowy moors.